Tracey Jane Jackson

Bound By Light

Book #7 in the Cauld Ane Series

Sale of this book without a front cover may be unauthorized. If this book is coverless, it may have been reported to the publisher as "unsold or destroyed" and neither the author nor the publisher may have received payment for it.

Bound by Light is a work of fiction. Names, characters, places, and incidents are the products of the author's imagination and are used fictitiously. Any resemblance to actual events, locales, or persons, living or dead, is entirely coincidental.

Cover Photo
Couple:
Tracey Jane Jackson

Landscape:
Stock Photo

Cover Art
Jackson Jackson

Cover Models
Alex Taylor
Nathalie Stimely

2015 Tracey Jane Jackson
Copyright © 2015 by Tracey Jane Jackson
All rights reserved.

ISBN: 978-1515302032

Published in the United States

I've followed Tracey Jane Jackson's Cauld Ane series from book one and am constantly impressed by the way her characters keep growing and developing. Her dialogue is realistic and witty and her fast-paced storylines keep the series progressing nicely. I've enjoyed each Bound book, but Bound by Dreams is my favorite so far. I can't wait to see what happens next! *Amanda Washington: Author of the Perseverance Series and the Chronicles of the Broken Series*

This series is one I will be getting paperbacks to keep on my LOVE bookshelf and one I will be rereading many, many times!! This deserves more than just 5+++ stars, but since it is the highest rating it will let me give, it will have to do. *Amazeballs Book Addicts*

Other books in the Cauld Ane Series

Bound by Blood
Cauld Ane #1

Bound by Fire
Cauld Ane #2

Bound by Secrets
Cauld Ane #3

Bound by Song
Cauld Ane #4

Bound by Dreams
Cauld Ane #5

Bound by Tears
Cauld Ane #6

Other books by Tracey Jane Jackson

The Bride Price
Civil War Brides Series, Book #1

The Bride Found
Civil War Brides Series, Book #2

The Bride Spy
Civil War Brides Series, Book #3

The Bride Ransom
Civil War Brides Series, Book #4

The Rebel Bride
Civil War Brides Series, Book #5

The Bride Star
Civil War Brides Series, Book #6

The Bride Pursued
Civil War Brides Series, Book #7

The Bride Accused
Civil War Brides Series, Book #8

The Brides United
Civil War Brides Series, Book #9

Acknowledgements

Ása Erlingsdóttir, thanks again for the Icelandic translations!

Alex and Nathalie...thanks for being pretty people almost kissing!

Thanks to Ellen and Amanda for the edits and critiques...you guys are amazing!

For My Readers

*You are the reason these books exist!
Thanks so much for all your support.*

CHAPTER ONE

SYDNEY WARREN HEARD the doorbell, turned off the stove, and made a dash for the front door. Her mother taught art classes at Ohlone Community two days a week and wasn't typically this late. Sydney was supposed to join her today, but had been down for the count with a nasty migraine, so her mom insisted she stay home and rest. Any progress with the migraine had been lost in the last couple of hours when her mom hadn't answered the dozen or so texts and voicemails Sydney had left.

Sydney pulled open the door, hoping that her mother's explanation would be a lost phone and keys, but what she found were two police officers standing on her porch, looking grim.

"Sydney Warren?" the older gentleman asked.

Sydney forced back tears as she nodded.

"I'm Officer Hill," he said, nodding to his female counterpart, "and this is Officer Montclair. I'm sorry, ma'am, but your mother has been in a car accident."

"Where is she?" she asked, feeling a modicum of relief. If it was an accident, she could deal with that. "I'll come right now."

"She's at the hospital."

"What do you mean at the hospital?" she challenged. "Why didn't they call me? Why did they send cops?"

"May we come in?" Officer Montclair asked.

Sydney hesitated for a second before stepping back and letting the officers inside.

"Let's find somewhere for you to sit down."

She lifted a shaky hand to her mouth. "I need to sit down?"

Officer Montclair nodded. "Yes, ma'am."

"Um, okay," she rasped, and headed into the front room, sitting in her mother's favorite chair. "How badly is she hurt?"

"I'm sorry, ma'am, but your mother's injuries were too extensive, and she didn't make it."

"What? I don't understand." Sydney swallowed. "I thought you said she was at the hospital."

"She is. I'm sorry; we can't give any more information." Office Montclair gave her a gentle smile. "The doctor will speak with you when you get there."

Sydney nodded woodenly, her mind numbing as shock set in. "I'll get my keys."

"Do you have anyone who can drive you?"

She shook her head.

"We'll take you, ma'am."

"How will I get back?"

"One of us will be happy to bring you back."

She swallowed hard. "I...I need to get my purse."

The officer nodded and Sydney walked in a haze to the kitchen, grabbing her purse and keys before sliding on her shoes and heading back to the front door. She followed the cops to their car. She could have been walking through water to an octopus chariot, as surreal as the situation felt.

Sydney was grateful the officers didn't speak to her on the ride to the hospital. By the time they arrived, she had half-convinced herself that they'd made a huge mistake and she'd prove it to herself, and them, before telling her mom all about her eventful day.

She checked her phone (again) and there was still no return call from her mom. She still hoped she'd walk into the room and find someone else there. One of the officers opened her door and she slid out, following him inside.

They led her down a hallway teaming with medical staff and into a room that was eerily quiet. A doctor met her right inside the door. He cleared his throat, but Sydney caught sight of the figure in the bed and rushed past him before he could speak.

"Mama," she whispered, her heart rate spiking. Her mother lay bloodied and bruised, a tube in her mouth, her chest rising and falling as a hissing sound echoed in the stark room. Sydney glanced over her shoulder. "She's breathing."

The doctor sighed. "We're keeping her heart beating because your mother is an organ donor, but there is no brain activity. I'm sorry."

Sydney stroked her mother's cheek as a tower of hopes crafted by denial began to crumble. "What happened?"

"Head-on collision," one of the police officers answered.

Outside of the trauma to her body, she looked so peaceful. How could she be gone? Sydney's world shattered silently as she sat beside her mother's body, watching her chest rise and fall as the machines kept her "alive."

"Are you her only relative?" the doctor asked. "Is there anyone else? Your father perhaps?"

With a mighty effort, Sydney turned her head to answer him. "My father died a while ago. It's just us. My uncle, my mother's brother, lives in England, but I'm the one who has power of attorney."

The doctor pulled a chair up to her and touched her shoulder. "I just need a signature on these forms to release her organs, but why don't you sit a while with her? We have a little time still."

Sydney nodded and sank into a seat. "I need to call my uncle," she rasped.

"No problem," he said. "I'll give you some privacy."

"Thanks," Sydney whispered, and pulled out her phone with a trembling hand.

* * *

Present day...

Sydney walked off the plane and into the loving arms of her aunt Clara. "Welcome, love!"

Sydney gave her a tired smile. "Thanks, Auntie."

With nothing left for her in California, Sydney had pulled up stakes and moved to London. After all, the death of her mother left her an orphan. A twenty-four-year-old orphan, but an orphan, nonetheless.

Aunt Clara hugged her. "You're probably knackered, eh? We'll head straight home and you can sleep. Your uncle will be home around six and we can talk."

Sydney nodded. "Is Lucy there?"

"She will be soon. She had a couple of classes today, but should be home around four." Her aunt smiled. "Come on, Burt's got the car idling at the curb. Dennis is waiting at luggage claim."

Sydney nodded and walked with her aunt toward baggage claim. She didn't know Burt or Dennis, but deduced they were part of her aunt and uncle's staff. Uncle Carville—Uncle Cary—was exceedingly wealthy. Over the years he'd found it necessary to put into place an extensive myriad of trusted house staff and security personnel who had been with him for years. This protection now extended to Sydney, since she would be living with them for a while.

Arriving at baggage claim, Sydney discovered Dennis waiting to pull her bags from the carousel. She smiled and introduced herself and then pointed out the three that came around quickly. As they waited for the final piece, she thought about how she could easily get used to this kind of pseudo-Kardashian-esque lifestyle.

"There it is," Sydney said, and pointed to the final and largest, green and blue tartan suitcase coming towards them.

"I've got it, miss," Dennis said, and pulled it off the carousel.

Seemingly out of nowhere, a young man jogged to them at Dennis's wave of a hand and grabbed two of the bags, while Dennis took the other two and then led Sydney and Aunt Clara to the car. A rather fit, white-haired man gave a slight bow and opened the back door as they approached. "Burt, this is Sydney." Aunt Clara slid into the car.

He smiled. "Lovely to meet you, miss."

"You too. Thanks." She followed her aunt and Burt closed the door.

"You should feel free to just rest and get acquainted with the staff over the next week or so, love," Aunt Clara said. "You're not obligated to do anything for a while. Give yourself some time to grieve properly and heal."

Sydney nodded. "Thanks, Auntie."

They sat in peaceful silence as Burt drove them from Heathrow to St. Peters Place in London. Her aunt and uncle lived in a spacious four-story townhouse they'd gutted and renovated twice in the last thirty years. Lucy and her brother also lived there, although Anson would be moving out soon, as his job was taking him to France.

Burt pulled the car up to the front of the house, and Aunt Clara and Sydney climbed out. Tears sprang to Sydney's eyes as she gazed at the house and felt the love and comfort of family it had always held for her.

"We've put you in the room next to Lucy," Aunt Clara said. "She wanted you close, but if you'd like to sleep somewhere else, you let me know."

Sydney smiled. "That's my favorite room—I love being next to her."

Her aunt chuckled. "Almost verbatim what she said."

Burt and Dennis started up the stairs with Sydney's luggage and Aunt Clara squeezed her hand. "Are you hungry, love, or would you like to sleep?"

"I slept a bit on the plane, so I think I'll go with hungry."

"Come on, then, I'm sure Leticia has prepared something delicious you can snack on."

Sydney followed Aunt Clara back to the kitchen and enjoyed a spread of cheese and cold cuts before heading to her room and falling into bed. For the first time in a long time, she fell asleep quickly, but as usual, couldn't stay asleep all night. She only managed two hours and spent the rest of the time attempting to read.

At what her family would consider a "respectable hour," Sydney showered in what was deemed the "small bathroom." It was just off her bedroom and probably bigger than a few studio apartments in San Francisco. She'd giggled when her aunt had apologized the first time she'd stayed.

The room was all marble—a claw-foot tub, shower that fit two, plus a toilet *and* bidet. Double sinks sat along a wall with two mirrored medicine cabinets above them. A large skylight in the ceiling flooded the room with natural light and could be opened via remote.

She headed down to the kitchen and found Lucy sitting at the dinette table, a gossip magazine open in front of her. Because of jet lag and the fact that Lucy had gotten home later than expected, Sydney hadn't seen her yesterday, so it was a long overdue reunion.

Lucy let out an excited squeal and rushed for Sydney, pulling her into a hug. "You're here, you're finally here."

"I'm here, cuzzie." Sydney giggled and hugged her back. She pulled away and shook her head. "Do you ever not look perfect?"

Lucy had dark, glossy, shoulder-length hair that swung perfectly in an asymmetrical style that Sydney couldn't have achieved without a constant hairstylist. Sydney's, on the other hand, was long and straight, and probably would be forever. She was way too chicken to cut it more than an inch at a time.

Lucy rolled her eyes. "Hello, pot, have you met kettle?" She tugged Sydney to the table. "Come and have some brekkie."

"What would you like, Sydney?" Leticia asked with a smile.

"I'm happy to make something."

"You know the rules, love," the cook said good-naturedly.

"Oh, fine." Sydney gave her a mock frown, secretly loving being banned from the kitchen for a few days. "I'd love an egg on toast, please. I'll get my own coffee if you have it."

Leticia chuckled. "It's in the pot."

Sydney poured a cup and then sat next to Lucy.

Lucy set her magazine aside and folded her hands on the table. "What do you want to do today?"

"Just hang out if you don't mind." Sydney sipped her coffee. "I need to sit down with your dad at some point and sort out the inheritance and money from the sale of the house, but I kind of want to pretend that I'm on vacation for a little while." She forced a smile to her face, hoping it met her eyes, and lowered her coffee cup to hide the shaking in her hand.

Lucy squeezed her arm and nodded. "Okay, so we'll hang out today and then tomorrow we'll be obnoxious tourists."

"That sounds perfect," Sydney said, hoping it sounded genuine.

"Do you need to stop at the bank?"

"No, I have my credit card and a hundred pounds in cash."

"Good," Lucy said, staring at her phone. "Stasia and Nadia said they'd love to join us."

"Oh, that would be fun!" Again with the overly happy tone.

"We don't have to."

"No, I want to. Really," Sydney assured her.

Lucy grinned and pulled out her phone. "I'll let them know."

Three hours later, Sydney, Lucy, Stasia, and Nadia walked into a cafe near the London Eye. The girls had tried to get Sydney to go on the Ferris wheel, but it was never going to happen. They argued through most of the line, ordering in between good-natured bickering.

"But it has the most amazing views," Nadia continued as they took their seats.

"And if you'd like to go up in that death trap, you can feel free to take a few photos for me," Sydney said.

"It's perfectly safe, cuz," Lucy piled on.

Sydney nodded. "It is if you watch from the ground."

Stasia giggled. "She wouldn't even go on the roller coasters with me when I was in the States. I was forced to go with one of her friends."

"Oh, yeah, you had *such* a hard time screaming and hanging on to the arm of one Topher Murray, rock star wannabe and general poor man's bad boy."

"He was nice."

"I know he was, which is why he isn't a real bad boy. He took you on all the scary rides, promising to protect you, and spent the whole time staring at your butt whenever you walked in front of him."

Stasia gasped. "He stared at my bum?"

"Yes, yes, he did."

She groaned. "Why didn't you tell me? I would have totally given him tongue if I'd known."

Lucy choked on her tea. "Anastasia!"

"What? I thought he wasn't interested, so I kissed him all chastely and crap."

Sydney giggled. "He was trying to be a gentleman because I told him if he wasn't, I would cut a certain appendage off."

"Well, why'd you go and do that?" Stasia demanded. "We could've had *way* more fun than we did."

"I don't think I want to know what 'more fun' would have entailed." Sydney took a bite of her sausage roll and shook her head.

"No, you really don't," Lucy agreed.

Stasia sighed. "He was so hot. Are you guys still friends?"

Sydney shrugged. "Facebook friends mostly. He moved to Australia for a girl, and I guess they broke up, but he stayed."

Stasia raised an eyebrow. "Hmm, maybe I should reach out. I love Oz, and I'm thinking Daddy owes me a little trip for my grades this past semester."

"Aren't you nearly twenty-four?" Sydney said.

"Yes, so?"

"Your dad still buys you trips for doing well on college courses?"

Stasia giggled. "Daddy buys me anything I ask for."

Sydney blinked back tears.

"Oh crap, sorry, love," Stasia rushed to say. "I'm sorry about your parents. I shouldn't have said that."

"No, it's okay."

Lucy reached over and took Sydney's hand, giving it a gentle squeeze.

"So, Topher," Sydney pressed. "Do you want me to connect you two?"

"Yes, that would be amazing."

Sydney nodded, the subject effectively changed. All in all, it was a good day spent with old friends, and Sydney was able to enjoy the moment. Win for her...for now.

* * *

A week later, Lucy arrived home from school and pulled Sydney into her bedroom and closed the door.

"Whoa, lady, you okay?" Sydney whispered.

Lucy's head bobbed up and down as she let out a quiet squeal.

"I met a boy."

"Seriously?" Sydney giggled. "Deets, please!"

"His name's Zach and he's American." She let out a girly sigh. "His accent is divine."

"Yeah, yeah, go on."

"Well, he's just transferred from his school in California, and we've been talking for a few days. We hit it off right away and today he asked me if I'd like to go out with him. Like a date, date, and I said yes. Oh my god, Sid, he's so cute. Dark hair, these yummy chocolate-brown eyes, and he's tall and a total beefcake."

Sydney shook her head. "Sounds just like your type."

"It's like I imagined him and he appeared before me."

"Maybe's he's a robot," Sydney retorted.

"With a really big schlo—"

"Lucy!"

"Not all of us aspire to be virginal, love. No judgment, just fact. It's been a dry year for me and I need a little relief."

Sydney felt heat creep up her cheeks. "I just haven't met the one yet. That's all."

"Like I said. No judgment," Lucy stressed. "Anyway, once Dad runs his little report on Zach, I'm hoping he'll release me from my gilded cage and let me go out with him."

"I'm sure he will."

"I can't wait for you to meet him! You're going to love him."

Sydney smiled. "I don't doubt it."

"It needs to be soon, okay?"

"Sure. How about this weekend?"

"That would be great. I'll talk to him about it and we'll make a plan."

"Can't wait."

Lucy slid off her bed. "Okay, I have a paper to finish. I'll see you at dinner."

Sydney grinned and watched her leave. She wondered if she'd ever be in a place to date casually, but she doubted it. One thing Sydney knew about herself was that she never did anything casually. It made her vulnerable and it got her hurt, but try as she might, she couldn't change that part of her. She cared about people too much. For now though, she was happy to live vicariously through Lucy and watch the drama that would certainly unfold.

CHAPTER TWO

THANE ALLEN STOOD in the middle of his spacious hotel suite in London and stared at his iPad. Today marked the first day of the promotional blitz for his new movie releasing in three weeks. He typically hated these things, but this time around, he had his costar, Charlotte MacMillan, with him for the duration. This meant his closest friend Niall was there since he was married to Charlotte and they were rarely out of each other's presence.

The movie had been a hard sell to Niall. Thane had to do quite a bit of convincing, because it was an epic historical romance, and that meant some serious kissing scenes.

Charlotte had beat out forty other women who auditioned for the part, partly because she was American, but mostly because she was an incredible actress and an "unknown," which is what the director wanted.

Niall's other concern had been his and Charlotte's daughter, Moira Faith. He was worried about leaving her with an on-site caregiver while they were on location, but Charlotte reminded him that parents went to work every day, and she assured him Moira wouldn't be neglected if both of them were close.

In the end, Niall had been hired to score the film and his band, Fallen Crown, had performed the theme song, which Niall had written and he and Charlotte had sung as a duet. This kept him involved throughout the filming and editing process and close enough to keep an eye on his beautiful wife.

So far, the preliminary reviews of the movie were positive, which didn't really matter much to Thane. It was all about box office sales and then DVD rentals and sales later. If the people didn't like it, the preliminary reviews didn't mean much.

Thane heard the beep of his lock and then his assistant pushed through the door, followed by a waiter with room service. "Good morning," Pamela said brightly.

"Morning, Pam," Thane said. "You're chipper this fine day."

She grinned. "Am I? I should work on that. I ordered breakfast for you. Niall and Charlotte will join you in ten minutes."

"You're a godsend, Pam."

"Perhaps I'm underpaid, then," she retorted.

Thane laughed. "We can discuss that at your review."

"I look forward to it." She tipped the waiter then scanned her iPad. "Do you want to go through the schedule now or eat first?"

"Schedule, I think."

"Right." She skimmed a finger over her screen as she sat in the chair by the window. "You and Charlotte will have fifteen-minute interviews with twenty-two media outlets. Niall will join you for the last five minutes of each one."

"Aye," Thane said, and studied his screen.

"Most of the interviewers you know, though there are a couple of new ones from America. Wallace says they're okay, and he's fully vetted them."

"Good work." Thane smiled. "What cold and exotic paradise am I sending you to when this circus is over? Did you get your fill of Siberia last time?"

Pam giggled. "Honestly, I just want to hang out at home in my pajamas for a couple of weeks."

"Fair enough."

A knock at the door had Pam rising to her feet. "I bet this is the MacMillans."

She opened the door and Charlotte and Niall walked inside, Niall carrying one-year-old Moira. Thane stood and greeted his friends while Pam went off to take care of a few things.

"Oh my gosh, I'm so nervous," Charlotte said, and flopped on the sofa next to Niall.

"Why?" Thane asked.

"Oh, I don't know. Maybe because this is my first film and I'm not a particularly interesting person. Why the heck would they want to interview me?"

Niall chuckled. "Because you're stunningly beautiful, exceedingly talented, and more fascinating than anyone else I know."

She snorted. "You have to say that. You're my mate."

Thane chuckled. "Well, *I'm* not your mate, and I wholeheartedly agree with Nye."

Charlotte blushed. "Thank you."

Niall pulled her close and kissed her temple, smiling at something she probably said to him telepathically. Thane focused on his coffee for a few seconds. He wondered if his mate was close. He was young compared to the majority of his friends. Less than three hundred years old, but it was a long time to wait for a mate and, he had to admit, he was getting restless.

The Cauld Ane had been rocked with surprises over the past few years. Their king had bound a human woman, as had both of the princes. Even Niall had bound a human, and Thane wondered if this was why he was waiting so long. Was his mate human as well?

"Thane?"

"Hmm?" He glanced at Niall.

"You all right, brother?"

Thane chuckled with a nod. "Aye. Sorry. My mind's elsewhere. What were we talking about?"

"Well, I'd like to know if there are any topics I should avoid," Charlotte said.

Moira wiggled her way out of Niall's arms and toddled to Thane. He picked her up and settled her on his lap.

"Just answer what you feel comfortable with," Thane said. "They're going to pry, but you're not obligated to talk about anything you don't want to. I think the biggest question will be how Nye felt about the kissing scenes."

"And the other parts," Charlotte grumbled, her face bright red.

Thane tried not to laugh at Niall's expression. "Aye. But you can tell them there was a body double."

"I don't know how I feel about that," she said.

"Why, love?" Niall challenged.

"I don't know." She shrugged. "It's not like there was nudity in the film, I guess, but I felt a little uncomfortable even alluding to it."

"You'd be surprised how often it happens," Thane said. "Don't worry about it. They probably won't even ask."

"Do you think it'll do well?"

Niall laughed. "Baby, it's a period piece with Thane Allen. It'll do very well."

She giggled. "I suppose that was a silly question."

"Let's finish our breakfast," Thane said. "We'll need our energy to deal with the jackals."

"Unca Thane, book, please?" Moira asked, and gave him a slightly toothless grin.

"I'd love to read you a book, lassie. Did Mummy bring one?"

"No, Mommy did not," Charlotte confessed.

"Never fear," Thane said, and grabbed his cell phone, sending a quick text to Pam. "Uncle Thane is on the job."

Niall grinned and sipped his coffee. Charlotte motioned Moira over and the little girl reluctantly left Uncle Thane's lap with the promise of food.

Pam arrived a few minutes later with one of Moira's favorite books and Moira climbed back onto Thane's lap for a quick story time.

Twenty minutes later, it was time to face the media, so Moira was handed off to her sitter, and Thane followed Pam into the suite set up for the interviews and took his seat. Charlotte sat beside him and gave him a nervous smile.

"You're going to do great, lass," he promised.

"Thanks."

Niall kissed her quickly and then stood off to the side.

A young blonde woman walked in and shook their hands. "Hi, I'm Christine Beach. Thanks so much for speaking with me."

"You're from Portland," Charlotte said. "You're on the KRTV news channel, right?"

"I am." Christine smiled. "I understand you're from Portland too, is that correct?"

"Yes," Charlotte said.

"Nice to meet you," Thane said.

"You too," Christine said. "Are you ready?"

Thane nodded. "Always."

"In this movie, you play an American. You did a great American accent, by the way."

Thane grinned. "Thank you."

"How hard was it to get into character, and did you ever find yourself slipping back into your Scottish accent?" Christine continued.

"I found the accent relatively easy; however, it was the pacing that was a little harder. Charlotte helped a great deal, and if I slipped, she'd correct me."

"You didn't slip very often," Charlotte said.

Thane chuckled. "Because of you."

She rolled her eyes. "Whatever."

"This story is about Sophie, a woman who is catapulted in time back to the American Civil War and you play Jamie, the husband who follows her. The chemistry between the two of you was hot, hot, hot. Were the love scenes difficult or is there a spark between you two also?"

"Considering the fact that my costar happens to be married to my closest friend," Thane said, "I can't say it was easy. But Charlotte's an incredible actress, so I can't say it was hard either."

Charlotte giggled. "I personally found it almost impossible to kiss Thane. I mean, look at him, he's so ugly."

Christine chuckled.

The interviews continued, the questions all relatively the same from interviewer to interviewer.

* * *

Sydney rushed into the hotel lobby to escape the rain and groaned. She was lost. Hopelessly lost. She was supposed to be meeting Lucy at a local coffee shop, but she'd made a wrong turn somewhere along the way, and then buckets of water had begun to fall from the sky, and she had no idea where she was now.

Gah! She was going to have to concede that she was directionally challenged and call her cousin.

Pulling out her cell phone, she shot off a text and rolled her eyes when Lucy called right back. "Don't say it," Sydney begged.

Lucy giggled. "I'm trying to figure out if it's an American thing, or just a Sydney thing."

"It's most definitely a Sydney thing," she admitted. "I was doing so well, but I stopped to get some money out of the ATM and I think that's where I went wrong. But you have to cut me some slack. I've only been here for a few weeks and London's a zoo. Who can expect anyone to find their way around?"

"Oh, love, you're doing great. Where are you?"

"The Ritz."

"Okay, why don't you stay where you are and I'll come and get you?" Lucy suggested.

Sydney sighed. "Probably a good idea. But wait for the rain to let up a little. I'm warm and dry, so I can hang out here for now."

"Alright," Lucy agreed. "I'll text you when I'm on my way."

"Miss?" Sydney turned to see a bellboy motioning to her. "You need to come with me, you're late."

"Luce, I have to go. See you when you get here." Sydney hung up.

"You really need to come with me now," the man insisted.

Sydney frowned. "I think you've got me confused—"

"Look, I don't mean to be rude, but you need to follow me or I could get sacked."

"I...ah. Okay," Sydney said. She had no idea what the guy was talking about, but maybe he knew something she didn't. She followed the man into the elevator and up to the tenth floor. She was ushered into a large hotel suite where a couple dozen other people milled around, some on phones, others on computers, but all looking very professional and important.

A young, attractive woman rushed toward her. "Are you the American?"

"Ah, well, I *am* American," Sydney confirmed.

"Oh, good. You're late."

"I am?"

"Yes," she said with an irritated sigh. "We're running behind now. Please follow me."

"I'm sorry, really. I think, but I—"

"Well, we can't cry over spilled milk now, can we," the woman said. "Come with me."

Sydney forced herself to stay calm. Dang it! She needed to learn to say no.

"Right this way." The woman pushed open a door and guided Sydney inside. She was blinded by bright lights. In a matter of seconds, she realized she was staring at only the biggest movie star on the face of the earth and the breath left her body.

Holy crap. I'm less than two feet in front of Thane Allen.

"This is Lana Jones from Ivory Hope Magazine."

"Miss Jones?" Thane smiled at her.

His sexy smile distracted her and it took a minute for Sydney to find her voice. "Um, no, actually, I'm not."

* * *

Thane's heart stopped in his chest. He took in the sight of his mate with her long dark hair and deep brown eyes. She was taller than most human women, probably five-foot-nine, and she was stunning.

"I'm sorry?" Pam asked.

"My name is Sydney Warren."

"Then why are you here?"

"I have no idea. The bellboy said he'd get fired if I didn't come with him."

Pam scowled. "Bloody hell."

"Pam," Thane warned, and rose to his feet.

"Look, this is ridiculous," Pam continued. "We pay a bloody fortune to keep the crazies from getting in and—"

"Excuse me?" Sydney snapped. "Listen here, lady, I am *not* a crazy! I was dragged here, obviously due to a misunderstanding, but I'm not a crazy anything…well, by medical standards anyway. I suppose there might be people in the world who think I'm nuts, but not in the way that you're implying."

Thane forced back a chuckle. His mate was funny *and* beautiful.

"If you'll just show me how to get out of here, I'll go," Sydney continued. "I'm supposed to be meeting my cousin."

"Just a moment," Thane rushed to say, and stepped toward Sydney, but Pam still stood between them. "Pam, I need a minute."

"But, we're running behind as it is," she argued. "You have a queue of reporters waiting to speak with you."

"And they will continue to wait," he said quietly. Pam nodded, lowering her head in contrition, and Thane closed the distance between him and the lovely Sydney. "May I borrow you for a moment?"

"I...um..." Sydney's expression grew a little wary. "I really do need to go."

"It won't take long," he said, and laid his hand on her lower back, the universal Cauld Ane action toward his mate. He closed his eyes, feeling the connection all the way to his soul.

"Okay," she whispered.

Thane guided her to the private room just out of sight and sound of the cameras and closed the door. He turned off his mic pack and smiled at her. "Don't worry, I won't hurt you."

"I'm not afraid of you." She raised an eyebrow. "I'm American. I carry mace."

Thane dropped his head back and laughed. "I thought that was a stereotype."

"Oh, fine." She let out an exaggerated sigh. "It's pepper spray."

"You really have pepper spray in your purse?"

"I feel as though I shouldn't answer that," she grumbled, holding her purse closer to her chest.

Thane grinned. "So, Sydney. Tell me about yourself."

"Um..." He could see she was fighting back nerves. "I wish I could, but I really do need to go. My cousin's meeting me here and if I'm not downstairs, she'll worry."

"Could I take you to dinner?"

"Dinner?" she asked, somewhat shocked. "Me?"

"Aye, lass. If you'll let me."

"Well, let's see." She crossed her arms. "You are Thane Allen, correct? *The* Thane Allen?"

"Last time I checked, aye."

"You're the biggest movie star on the planet, demanding the highest paycheck in the business right now, and haven't had a bomb since you hit the scene."

Thane smiled. She'd apparently read the latest *People* magazine. "So I'm told."

"And you want to take *me* to dinner?"

"Aye, love."

She narrowed her eyes. "Why?"

"Why not?"

"Because we've never met, you're a movie star, I'm an American here visiting my family...and you're a movie star."

He laughed. "Aye, lass, but that's what I do. It's not who I am. I happen to think you're beautiful and I never pass up the opportunity to get to know someone beautiful."

"You never pass up the opportunity, huh? Your dinner schedule must be pretty booked, then. So I'll just go ahead and—" She took a step toward the door.

"Wait. That's not what I mean." He dragged his hands down his face. "I'm sorry. That made me sound like an arse."

Sydney bit her lip. "A bit of a player, maybe, but not an ass."

He smiled. "I promise I'm not a player."

"Which is exactly what a player would say."

"Go to dinner with me," he pled.

"What if I'm an ax murderer?" she countered. "I could be a really beautiful ax murderer and if you take me to dinner, the world will lose an international treasure."

"You think I'm a treasure?"

"You are on the big screen, but I don't know what you're like in real life. I don't believe everything I read, so I tend to reserve judgment on people who have publicists."

Thane watched her in fascination as she grew more animated by the second. A beautiful pink covered her cheeks. "Sorry, I'm rambling. I think it's really nice that you would like to take me out to dinner, but—"

"Before you say no," he interrupted.

"No."

"*Before* you say no," he repeated, "will you think about it? I'll give you my number and you can ring me."

She let out a quiet snort. "I'm not going to call *the* Thane Allen."

"Why not?"

"Because you're...well, you're...you. This is just insane."

"Is it?" Thane was beginning to feel a little insecure. Why was it so difficult to convince his mate, the woman he was destined to be with until death, to go to dinner with him?

"Wait..." Sydney cocked her head to the side. Her expression grew guarded. "Did Lucy put you up to this?"

Lucy? "I'm sorry, lass, but I don't know who Lucy is."

"Is this like that one time when you took those orphans to that Fallen Crown concert? And now, you're being sweet because of my situation..." Her voice caught and tears formed in her eyes. She blinked them away.

What bloody situation?

"You don't have to do this. It's very sweet, but not necessary. I'll tell Lucy you tried." She pulled out her phone and shook her head. The pain in her eyes made him want to go to her, to hold her and make everything better.

Not wanting to confuse her more, he held his ground. "Nobody put me up to anything. I just want to take you to dinner."

Sydney gave him a dismissive wave of her hand. Her smile looked forced. "You know what? You're as good an actor off-screen as on. Has anyone ever told you that?"

Something was wrong with his mate, and he couldn't fix it if she wouldn't even let him take her to dinner. He'd never worked this hard for a date. He'd never worked for a date, *period*. Hoping he didn't sound as desperate as he felt, he said, "How about you give me your number and I'll give you a ring?"

The door opened and Pam said, "Thane, we really need to get a move on?"

He turned to her. "Just give me a minute."

"We don't have a minute."

"I'll just get—" He turned back to Sydney, but she was gone. "Damn it." He rushed into the hallway, but he couldn't see her in the throng of people.

"Thane! Can we get a photo?"

"Thane, over here!"

Shite! He'd lost her. He smiled as best he could at the reporters, covering a river of bubbling frustration, and then slipped back into the private suite.

CHAPTER THREE

As SOON AS Thane was distracted, Sydney rushed out of the room and into the elevator, pressing the lobby button multiple times. Her cousin had to be the sweetest person in the world, and it would be just like Lucy to set Sydney up in order to lift her spirits. But it was a pity date, and only made her feel pitiful. How the heck did Lucy know Thane Allen anyway? Sydney's aunt and uncle had money, which meant they had connections; maybe Lucy contacted him through one of them.

The doors popped open and she walked to the lobby, finding Lucy in the sea of faces. Her cousin rushed toward her. "There you are! I thought you'd left."

"Sure you did."

"I just got here. Are you okay?"

"Yeah. I'm okay. Really, I am. Look, what you tried to do was sweet and all, but..."

"What the devil are you talking about, Sid?" Lucy demanded, seeming to be genuinely confused.

"The whole Thane Allen thing."

"What Thane Allen thing?"

Suddenly Sydney wasn't so sure about her cousin's involvement. "Oh, come on, Luce. It's blown. You really expect me to believe that Thane Allen asked me to dinner, and you had nothing to do with it?"

"What the—?"

Sydney waved her hand. "It's all good. I figured it out. Like I said, sweet, but not necessary."

"Hold on a tick." Lucy grabbed Sydney's arm and pulled her to a stop. "Thane Allen's here? In this hotel and he asked you to dinner?"

"Yeah. But you knew that. You set it up."

"I bloody well did not! If I was going to set anyone up with Thane Allen, it would be me!"

"Lucy, quit messing around."

Lucy scowled. "Sydney Roslyn Warren, I am quite literally *not* messing around. Did you or did you not meet Thane Allen, and did he or did he not invite you to dinner? For real?"

Oh, crap! Sydney's heart raced. "I really met him and he really asked me to dinner."

"Oh, my giddy aunt," Lucy breathed out with a groan. "What did you say?"

"I told him he was a really good actor. Onscreen and off." Sydney swallowed with a grimace. "I thought I was being set up. I thought it was a pity date."

"Sydney! You didn't!" Lucy wailed. "Bloody hell, love, you are the daftest woman I've ever met."

"You really didn't put him up to it?" Sydney asked as she wrung her hands.

"And exactly how the hell would I have put Thane Allen up to it, Sid? Oh, my *god*, just because we live under the rule of the same queen does not mean we all know each other!"

"I never said you did," Sydney grumbled.

Lucy pointed to the elevator. "You need to go back and accept."

Sydney's mouth dropped open. "I am *not* running back upstairs and begging him to take me out, Lucy. Let's just go home."

"The sexiest man alive just asked you out, are you really going to blow him off?"

"What possible reason would the sexiest man alive have to want to take me out, Lucy? It's ridiculous."

Lucy crossed her arms. "Maybe he thinks you're gorgeous."

"Then maybe he's blind."

"You're an idiot, lovie. Truly."

Sydney rolled her eyes. "I'm starving. Let's just get home, okay?"

"I'm going to talk to Dad and see if he can get in touch with him."

"No you're not!" Sydney squealed. "Please, Lucy, don't okay?"

"Fine." Lucy sighed. "I think you're insane, but fine."

"Thanks. Now, lead me home."

Lucy giggled and they headed toward the Tube.

They arrived home to an empty house, and Sydney decided some cooking therapy was on her list today. She had to find something to distract her from her strange encounter. "Luce!" she called up the stairs. "Spaghetti and meatballs sound good?"

"Sounds amazing!" Lucy called back. "Need some help?"

"No, I'm quite capable of setting the house on fire all by myself."

Sydney grinned at Lucy's four-letter response. Lucy couldn't even boil water, which blew Sydney's mind. Even though both families had plenty of money, the cousins couldn't have been raised more differently. Sydney did her own laundry, cooked twice a week when she was home, and contributed to the household chores. Lucy, not so much. The Ashworths had a live-in housekeeper, along with Leticia, who provided meals six days a week. Tonight was her night off, so Sydney was taking her chance to get in the kitchen.

She grabbed her iPod, cued it up to the new Fallen Crown album, and got her groove on while she seasoned and rolled out meatballs. For the first time in a long time, she was feeling a sense of relief. She'd felt it when Thane had touched her and now she felt it again. Strange, but she wasn't going to question it too much. It was a nice feeling. One she'd like to get used to.

Once the meatballs were formed and cooked, she made her magic sauce, and then boiled the pasta. She and Lucy had a quiet dinner, albeit fancy since Lucy insisted on setting the table with the good china, and then Sydney powered up her Kindle and got lost in a book.

Tonight was the first night in forever was determined to actually relax. Turn off her brain enough to enjoy an epic historical saga. Maybe she'd even sleep. It would be bliss.

* * *

"Sydney Warren," Thane said as he paced his hotel room. "All I know is that she's American." *And she's in trouble.*

"That's not much to go on," Niall said.

They'd just finished their interviews and were now back in Thane's suite discussing the events of the day.

"Have you tried to speak with her... you know, telepathically?" Charlotte asked.

"Aye. I can't quite find her thought pattern."

"Is this her?" Charlotte asked, and turned her laptop to face Thane.

He leaned down to see the screen. "Yes! How did you do that?"

She giggled. "It's called a Facebook search."

Thane sat down and took the computer from her, scrolling through Sydney's profile. "Damn, it's set to private. I can only see her profile picture and her friends."

Charlotte waved her hand toward him. "Hit the friend request button. If she accepts it, then I'll be able to see more and reach out to her."

"Done," he said, and handed the laptop back.

"You really don't have a Facebook page?"

"Not a private one," he admitted. "My team handles all my social media pages and such."

Charlotte rolled her eyes and closed her computer. "You and Niall are so old."

"You may want to hide yours before this movie hits, Charlotte," Thane warned. "If you don't, you could run the risk of people finding out things about you that you'd rather stay private."

Niall picked up the computer and began hitting keys.

"Nye, what are you doing?" Charlotte asked.

"Hiding your profile," Niall said.

"What? What do you mean?" Charlotte gasped, grabbing for the computer. "You can't just unfriend people, Nye."

"I didn't," he said.

She frowned at the screen. "Gah! You shut down my account?"

"It's safer."

She glared at him and Thane knew she was yelling at him telepathically. Niall raised an eyebrow at one point and then Charlotte blushed beet red.

"Really, Nye? You're unbelievable," she snapped.

He chuckled. "I know, baby."

"I hear your concerns," she said carefully. "But I just sent a request to Sydney. If my account is disabled, she won't be able to respond."

Niall stared over at Thane. "You have a man, right?"

"Aye."

Niall smiled and turned back to Charlotte. "Thane's man will find her."

She rose to her feet, closing the laptop as she did. "Excuse us, Thane. I need to verbally spank my husband and would rather not have an audience."

"Moira's next door, love," Niall pointed out.

She let out a frustrated groan. "And she can hang with her sitter for a few extra minutes."

Niall chuckled.

Charlotte gave Thane a saccharin smile. "Sorry, Thane, I have a man to murder."

Thane choked back a laugh and nodded. "Don't let me stop you."

She headed for the door and Niall rose slowly to his feet, a goofy grin on his face. "Have a great day, brother."

"You as well."

Thane watched as Niall followed his mate and shook his head. Niall had changed. He was the epitome of a good man. He always had been. It kind of made up for the actions of his brother, Max, who was somewhat of a loose cannon. Niall was the nice guy, the one who never lost his temper, and the one who had patience in spades. But when Niall met Charlotte, he suddenly had an edge. Not one that made him difficult, just one that made him sharper. Charlotte had a unique set of gifts and if Niall had been a lesser man, their marriage could have been disastrous.

Thane smiled and grabbed his cell phone. It was time to call his "man."

"Hello, Thane," Wallace said, cheerily. "What can I do for you?"

Thane chuckled. "Actually, I'm wondering if you can find someone for me."

"Of course I can. Who?"

"I don't have much." He rubbed his forehead. "A name and nationality…general description, that sort of thing."

"No worries. Just give me what you have."

Thane gave Wallace what he knew and then moped around the hotel suite while he waited. The London premiere was in two days and tomorrow would be full of more interviews and press before he'd get a break. Once the premiere was done, he could go home; however, it was the first time in a very long time that he wasn't interested in escaping to his cottage. Right now, he wanted to find his mate and go about wooing her so they could go home together.

He poured a glass of whiskey and stood at the window overlooking Piccadilly. His thoughts turned to Sydney again, wondering where she was. He couldn't imagine she was far if she'd ended up in his hotel. At least, not so far he couldn't get to her relatively quickly.

Dropping his forehead to the cool glass, he closed his eyes and focused. Maybe if he could settle his mind, he might be able to speak with her. His natural gift of empathy should give him that ability, but he wasn't sure how it worked with a human.

He didn't have long to try as his phone buzzed in his pocket seconds later. "Yes."

"I can't find her," Wallace said.

"What?" Thane asked.

"She's either some kind of a computer hacker or someone's hiding her. She doesn't really exist."

"How the hell does she not exist?" Thane snapped. "Charlotte found her on Facebook in a matter of seconds."

"Well, she's not on Facebook anymore."

"Shite." Thane rubbed his forehead.

"I'll keep looking, but I doubt we'll find anything today. I'll call you as soon as something changes."

"Right. Thanks."

Thane hung up with a frown. Grabbing his drink, he flopped onto the sofa and continued to try to connect with the elusive Sydney Warren the old-fashioned, non-technical Cauld Ane way.

* * *

The next morning, Sydney knocked on her uncle's office door and entered when bid. Uncle Cary was a large man with salt-and-pepper hair and a deep voice that both terrified and comforted most people, depending on his mood.

"Good morning, love," he said, and rose to his feet, hugging Sydney gently. "How did you sleep?"

"Okay." She sat in the chair opposite his and smiled. "I think I'm ready for all this yuckiness."

"It's not so bad, Sid. I promise. Your parents organized everything remarkably well, so you have several options. One of which is to do nothing, at least for the moment."

"Ooh, I like that option."

Her uncle chuckled. "I had a feeling you'd say that, so I gathered all the information and saved it here." He handed her a flash drive and a manila file. "Plus I printed everything out. Should you have any questions, let me know."

"You're a lifesaver, Uncle Cary. Thank you."

"Anytime, love. Now, we need to talk about something else, something you might find a little invasive."

Sydney settled the file on her lap. "Okay."

"I have disabled your social media accounts."

"Why?"

"Because you need to be invisible for a while." He frowned as he took a deep breath. "Also, I have let Lucy know and she's a bit annoyed with me, but you will need to have security with you anytime you leave the house."

"Seriously? Why?" Sydney bit her lip. "Am I in danger?"

"We don't think so. Right now, it's a precaution."

"A precaution?" she challenged. "Uncle Cary, tell me. Did something happen?"

"Nothing I can talk about at the moment. Will you trust me? At least for a little while?"

"Um...I guess." Sydney had no reason *not* to trust him and it wasn't like this never happened. She remembered Lucy complaining about tightened security a few years ago when her dad was making a big merger. There'd been death threats and Uncle Cary had hired bodyguards for both Lucy *and* Anson.

He gave her a bolstering smile. "I know it's a pain, but you'll find you forget they're even there."

Sydney rolled her eyes. "I'm not so sure about that."

"Humor an old man, eh?"

"Do you think it'll be a permanent thing?"

"No, love, I don't. But it's permanent for now," he admitted.

Sydney sighed. "What if I meet some dashing Brit who sweeps me off my feet? I can't have some strange man following me on dates."

Uncle Cary chuckled. "We'll cross that bridge when we get to it."

"Okay." She smiled, begrudgingly. "Thank you for everything, Uncle Cary. I really appreciate it." Sydney wasn't sure that was sincere, but since she was in her uncle's home, she would trust him.

"Don't mention it, sweetheart. You know you've always been like another daughter to me. You are the very best of my sister, you know. You remind me so much of her."

Sydney blinked back tears. "Thanks. I often wished Anson and Lucy were really my brother and sister. You guys were always so close and I wanted that."

"We *were* close, but you feel free to torture Anson just as much as your mother tortured me. Lucy's far too nice to him."

Sydney giggled. "I'll keep that in mind."

"Good." He rose to his feet. "Lucy mentioned something about a Thane Allen movie premiere tomorrow night?"

"She did?" Sydney began to think of ways to commit cousincide as she stood. "What did she say?"

"Just that she wanted to go." Her uncle cocked his head. "Why?"

Sydney relaxed. "Oh, nothing."

He hummed in suspicion. "Anyway, I've wrangled a few tickets if you'd like to go."

"Oh, wow, that sounds fun."

"We'll make it a family outing." Uncle Cary grinned. "Dinner first?"

"Perfect."

"Good. I'll have my assistant set everything up."

"Can't wait."

Sydney hugged her uncle again and then went to look for Lucy.

* * *

The next evening, the house was awash with excitement. Sydney had never been to a movie premiere before and felt her stomach flutter with nerves as she and Lucy dressed in cocktail dresses and their favorite heels.

The premiere was being held at the Empire Cinema in Leicester Square and the family had the choice to walk the red carpet with the celebrities or enter before they descended. A resounding agreement was reached to skip the circus and sneak in early, so they had to be out the door in less than an hour.

"I wonder if he'll ask you out again," Lucy mused.

Sydney ignored the shiver that thought created. "I doubt we'll even see him."

"It's very possible we'll sit quite close to him."

"No!" Sydney gasped. "Really?"

Lucy giggled. "Really. It's an intimate event on celebrity event scales."

"Why did you do this, Luce? Maybe I should just stay home."

"No way. Look at it as a nice family outing and if we see the famous and gorgeous Thane Allen, then it's a bonus." She raised an eyebrow. "Besides, you're probably right. We probably won't see him...but if we do, I doubt we'll interact with him."

"Exactly." Sydney took a deep breath and nodded. "Okay. Cool."

Lucy laughed. "Why do you get so nervous around boys, Sid?"

"Um, *hello*, he's not just a boy, Luce. He's Thane Allen, and I was kind of rude before, so I'm half expecting him to shun me and tell the world what a cow I am."

"You're ridiculous."

Sydney shrugged. "Hopefully, if he sees me, he'll just ignore me."

"There's the spirit." Lucy grinned.

"What about you? No Zach tonight?"

Lucy and Zach had been exclusive for just over a week now and she was still basking in the new love glow. Sydney had yet to meet him, mostly because he wanted to wait to meet Lucy's family until they were "more secure." Sydney couldn't quite decide if she liked that or not, but figured Lucy would make it happen when she wanted it to happen.

"Dad could only get tickets for the five of us," Lucy said.

"He can have mine," Sydney offered.

"Nice try." Lucy giggled. "Shall we?"

Sydney shook off her nervousness and grabbed her jacket and purse. She followed Lucy downstairs and into the waiting car with the rest of the family.

CHAPTER FOUR

THANE ADJUSTED HIS bowtie and smoothed down his tuxedo jacket. He was surprisingly excited about the event tonight, even with the weight of success on his shoulders. He'd financed the majority of this project and if it failed, he'd take the hit.

Pam arrived with Niall and Charlotte in tow. Charlotte wore a corseted modernized version of one of the gowns she'd worn in the film. It had been her favorite and the deep blue matched her eyes perfectly.

Thane kissed her cheek. "You look beautiful, Charlotte."

"Thank you." She sighed with a grin. "I feel like a princess."

Niall pulled her close and kissed her temple.

"Where are Max and Grace?" Thane asked.

"They're going with the band," Niall said. "I offered to go with them as well—"

"But I need you with me," Charlotte rushed to say.

"Which is why I'm here." Niall chuckled. "So, breathe..."

She took a deep breath. "Thank you, honey."

"Where's the baby?" Thane asked.

"With Megan," Charlotte said.

"Some lovely grandmother, granddaughter time, then."

"Exactly."

"Car's downstairs," Pam said as she walked back into the room.

"Ready?" Thane asked.

Charlotte clapped her hands. "Yes. I'm nervous and excited all at the same time."

Thane grinned. "I am as well, lass."

He and Niall stepped back and let Charlotte precede them out of the hotel. It took a few minutes to get her and her dress loaded into the limo, but they made it and headed to the theater.

* * *

"Mmm, champagne and popcorn," Sydney murmured somewhat sarcastically. "My favorite."

"Champagne with just about anything works for me," Lucy added, and took a sip. "Especially when it's good."

Lucy's parents and brother were on the opposite side of the cinema lobby speaking with an acquaintance of her father's, so Lucy had pulled Sydney over to the refreshments. Neither of them were particularly interested in the fascinating conversation of finance and the world economy.

"When do we get to sit down?" Sydney stepped from one foot to the other. "My feet are starting to scream at me."

"Mine as well. I can't imagine it will be long now. It's almost seven."

Before Lucy could get the words completely out of her mouth, the roar of the crowd outside grew and Sydney figured the stars were arriving. They'd gone through thirty minutes of the lesser known actors of the film, but now was the moment the crowd outside had been waiting for. "Let's go somewhere else," Sydney whispered.

"Where?"

"It doesn't matter. We can join your parents. I just don't necessarily want to be in the way."

Lucy shook her head. "We have a chance to be within spitting distance of both Fallen Crown *and* Thane Allen. I'd very much like to be in the way."

"I had no idea you had llama tendencies."

Lucy giggled. "Nice."

Sydney smiled and stepped behind Lucy in an effort to hide... hard to do when she was almost two inches taller than her cousin. Her hands were shaking, so she set her drink down on the counter and linked her fingers together in front of her.

She couldn't help but get caught up in the excitement as the band members filed in, and when Max MacMillan arrived, she felt her heart race and found herself star struck. He had one of the most amazing voices in the world and was drop-dead gorgeous to boot. His wife was stunning as well with her dark hair swept into an ornate up-do. Although he took time to sign autographs and speak with fans inside, he was never far from her. It was very sweet.

Lucy giggled and craned her head to look at Sydney. "Here comes Thane."

Sydney bent her knees and peeked over Lucy's shoulder, trying to be as inconspicuous as possible, but was still unable to stop herself from watching him walk in. Truly, the man was beautiful with the soft stubble over his jaw and his thick, dark strawberry-blond hair. She wanted to run her hands through it.

He was speaking with his costar, Charlotte, and her husband, Niall, the drummer for Fallen Crown, and Sydney felt the sudden need to escape.

"I'm going to the restroom," she whispered, and dashed away from the crowd. Lucy followed and they spent a few minutes pretending to fix their already perfect makeup. Sydney hoped it was long enough in order to sneak in just before the movie started.

Lucy checked her watch. "Two minutes, love. We should really get in there."

Sydney nodded and squared her shoulders, leading Lucy from the bathroom. They walked toward the theater and as they stepped through the door, Sydney stalled.

"I wondered if I'd see you again," Thane whispered. He was standing just inside, leaning against the wall. He pushed away with a smile. "You're difficult to find, Sydney Warren."

Sydney chewed on her bottom lip, dumbstruck.

"I'm Lucy." Lucy stuck her hand out and Thane shook it.

"You're the cousin?" Thane asked.

"I am," she said. "It's lovely to meet you."

"Lovely to meet you too, lass."

Sydney stood frozen to her spot on the carpet, unable to form a coherent sentence as her cousin and crush carried on a pleasant conversation.

"Sid?" Lucy squeezed her arm.

"Hmmm?" she mumbled.

"I'm going to find the fam. I'm sure Thane can make sure you find a seat?" Lucy made it both a statement and a question, which didn't really help Sydney's nerves.

"I'd be happy to," Thane said.

"I should come with you," Sydney managed to say.

"No, love, you stay," Lucy argued. "I'll save you a seat."

"But the movie's going to start."

"It won't start until I sit down," Thane said.

"Have a little fun, cuz," Lucy whispered, and kissed her cheek before walking away and out of her sight.

Sydney bit her lip again and stared at the movie star. Good Lord, he was gorgeous, especially up close.

"Hi," he said, and smiled.

"Hi." She took a deep breath. "How did you know I'd be here?"

"I didn't," he said. "But I saw you rush away when I came in, so I waited. Will you sit with me tonight?"

"What?" She let out a quiet gasp. "I couldn't."

"Why not?" he challenged.

"Because you're the star of the movie and I'm a nobody. What will people think?"

He chuckled. "I've never much cared about what other people think, lass. It's served me well in life. At least so far."

"I'm here with my family, though. It would be rude."

"How about you introduce me and I'll ask them directly?"

Sydney narrowed her eyes. "Do you ever take 'no' for an answer?"

"Not when I'm in the strange position of having to convince a beautiful woman to sit with me in a movie theater."

Sydney shivered. Lordy, he was sexy. "Aren't they waiting on you to start?"

"Aye, lass they are, but we can stand here all night if you'd like to."

He gave her another sexy little grin that caused her to blush. "Oh, for the love and glory be. Come on, I'll introduce you to my family."

"Excellent idea." Thane held his arm out and she slid her hand around it.

They walked into the large theater. All eyes were suddenly on them and Sydney instantly wanted to run away. Thane laid his free hand over hers and gave it a squeeze as he led her to a very official looking woman, headphone and microphone on. As they got closer, Sydney recognized her from the hotel, complete with impressive glare aimed at Thane.

Before the woman could say anything, he raised a hand. "I know, Pam. Just give me one more minute and I'll be ready."

She sighed and nodded as Sydney found her family in the crowd.

"Ready, love?" he whispered.

Sydney nodded and led him up the stairs. Her aunt was aflutter as Thane introduced himself, and Sydney felt a little embarrassed by all the attention.

"I do hope you won't mind if I steal Sydney for the rest of the evening," Thane said, still holding her aunt's hand.

"Of course not," she said. "She's all yours."

Sydney noticed he waited to release Aunt Clara's hand until Uncle Cary nodded his approval.

"Thank you." Thane faced Sydney and smiled. "Shall we?"

"Um, sure."

He linked his fingers with hers, guiding her to his seats in the front. Sydney thought she might die of nervousness right then and there. Next to Thane sat Niall MacMillan, then Niall's wife and Thane's costar, Charlotte, then Max MacMillan's wife, Grace, then Max. Oliver Bardsley, the bass player from Fallen Crown was next to him. Henry Keys, the keyboardist, and his wife and older children sat in the row in front.

She noticed the men stood as she sidled to her seat and was surprised to be pulled into a warm hug by Charlotte. "Hi Sydney. Thane hasn't been able to shut up about you."

"You're American."

Stupid, stupid, stupid thing to say!

Sydney felt heat creep up her neck. "Sorry, that was dumb."

"Not at all." Charlotte giggled. "Portland, Oregon. Until this one swept me off my feet." She pointed to Niall, who shook Sydney's hand.

"Lovely to meet you lass," Niall said.

"You too," Sydney said, and smiled at Charlotte. "I love Portland."

"It's a gorgeous city, for sure," Charlotte agreed, and after she'd introduced Sydney to Max and Grace, took her seat.

Sydney did the same and once everyone was seated, the lights dimmed and the movie began. She was surprised to find that she liked...no, *loved*...the way Thane held her hand throughout the film. And what a film it was. She had to admit, it was very surreal watching intense love scenes while sitting in between the two who were acting out said love scenes. If she didn't know better, she'd swear these two would give their lives for each other. Their chemistry was off the charts.

Thane's character, Jamie Ford, knelt at the empty bed of his missing wife and whispered, *"Where is she? Where is my wife?"* and thus began the emotional roller coaster that Sydney was strapped into for the next two hours and four minutes.

She was completely swept up in the story of the couple sent back to the Civil War as they miraculously find their way back to each other. She found herself gripping the armrest or gasping aloud, especially when Richard Madden tried to take advantage of his friendship with Sophie. Then when Sophie saw Jamie and he didn't recognize her, Sydney was devastated. She was a little embarrassed when Thane offered her his handkerchief. "Thank you," she sniffed.

He gave her hand a squeeze, lifting it to his lips after she dabbed at her eyes, trying to avoid smearing her makeup.

Throughout the rest of the movie, she barely managed to keep her emotions at bay. Luckily, she kept her sobbing to a very quiet internal struggle; the copious amount of tears pouring down her face were the only indication she was moved. As the credits rolled, she took advantage of the dark and pulled herself together.

The lights came up and the crowd gave a rousing round of applause. Thane leaned close and asked, "Will you stay here?"

Sydney nodded and he rose to his feet, helped Charlotte to her feet, and guided her down to the front.

Thane raised his hands and waited for the din to quiet down. "Thank you so much for joining Charlotte and me for the premiere. We are grateful you came and would love to hear your thoughts... unless they're negative, of course."

The group responded with laughter and more clapping.

"My assistant is probably going to kill me because we have a reception to get to, but does anyone have any questions?" he continued.

An older gentleman stood. "Thane, what did you like the most about your character, Jamie Ford?"

"I liked his absolute devotion to Sophie. Even when he didn't remember her, he still felt committed to her in his heart. He was sensitive, but didn't lose his sense of being a man."

"So you liked that he wasn't whipped," the man said.

Thane chuckled. "Exactly."

A young woman stood and smiled. "This question is for both of you. Do you feel a connection with the character you played? And was there anything you didn't like about your characters?"

"You first, lass," Thane said.

"Hmmm." Charlotte hummed in thought. "I definitely felt a deep connection with Sophie. This is a woman who was thrown back in time and, although she was passionate about that period in history, she was without the only man she'd ever loved. I've only been married to my husband for a couple of years and I couldn't imagine losing him even after a hundred years together, so I could feel her pain on a deep level. There wasn't much I didn't like about her, really. Except that at times I felt she forgot where she was and spoke a little more plainly than might have been wise." She smiled at Thane. "Your turn."

Thane stared at Sydney and a slow smile spread over his face. "The struggle I had with Jamie was that it took him a long damn time to find his woman and when he *did* find her, he didn't remember her. I know that if my wife walked up to me, I'd know her with every beat of my heart and every breath of my soul. When you find the one you're supposed to be with forever, you don't forget."

Sydney's heart raced as he spoke directly to her and the crowd let out a collective sigh at his words. Sydney licked her lips and closed her eyes for a brief moment to compose herself.

Thane and Charlotte graciously took questions for almost thirty minutes before Thane's assistant called a stop to the Q&A time.

"Alright, folks, please feel free to file out and help yourselves to food and beverages. It is an open bar tonight, so we'll have taxis at the ready to drive you home should you need it," Pam announced.

"We'll wait here until the crowd's out," Niall told Sydney. "Everyone wants a chance to meet the stars."

"Good plan." Sydney shifted to face him. "How do you handle watching your wife kissing another man?"

"I close my eyes," he admitted. "And then I kiss her over and over again so she never forgets who her real man is."

Sydney smiled. "I'm pretty sure she couldn't forget if she tried."

He chuckled and Sydney watched the guests walk by Thane and Charlotte as they filed out to the reception. Her family waved to her as they passed her seat, but didn't stop to chat, and then the room was empty and Thane came to collect her.

"Sorry, love," he said, and held his hand out to her.

"Don't be sorry." Sydney smiled as she took his hand and stood. "It was fascinating watching everything."

"Do you want to get out of here?"

"Don't you need to stay?"

"Not if I don't want to."

Sydney raised an eyebrow. "Really?"

He chuckled. "Okay, I should stay, but I'd rather go somewhere with you."

"That's sweet."

"It's not bloody sweet, love." He sighed. "It's the truth."

Sydney giggled. "Still sweet."

"Cheeky." He kissed her palm and smiled. "I'll have to take you out tomorrow night to make up for it."

"Don't do anything on my account."

"You don't want me to take you out?"

"That's not what I'm saying." Sydney shook her head and took a deep breath. "It's just that you unhinge me in a way."

He chuckled. "Good."

"Good?"

"Aye. Because you slay me, love, so if I can have a fighting chance with you, I'm on the right path."

Sydney folded her lips between her teeth and then smiled. "You can have a fighting chance."

He leaned down and kissed her cheek. "Bloody hell, love, you're adorable."

That was the last chance they got to speak for the next hour. When Sydney's family was ready to leave, she wasn't sure if she should say something to Thane or just walk out. She chose to walk out, but was stopped by Niall. "I'm going to grab him."

"You don't need to do that," Sydney said.

"He'd want me to. Believe me." Niall smiled at Sydney's uncle. "Would you please give us a moment? I won't keep her long."

"I can do that," Uncle Cary said.

"Thanks." Niall cupped Sydney's elbow and guided her to the crowd surrounding Thane. "Sorry folks, I just need to steal Thane for a moment."

Thane smiled and shook a few hands before stepping from the group and taking Sydney's hand. "You're not leaving, are you?"

"I am. My family's waiting, so I should go."

"I'm sorry I've neglected you, love."

"You haven't," she argued. "This was your night; I'm the one who crashed it."

"So..." He smiled and stroked her cheek. "Can I take you out tomorrow?"

"I think that will work."

"Excellent." He pulled out his phone and handed it to her. "Put your contact information in here and I'll give you a ring."

Sydney glanced over at her uncle, who was watching intently. He gave her a nod, so she entered her cell phone number and handed the phone back to Thane. He moved his fingers over the screen. "I just sent you a text. You now have my information. I'll trust you not to share."

She widened her eyes. "Oh, I wouldn't."

"I know, love. I'm joking." He smiled. "Are you a night owl or an early riser?"

She shrugged. "I don't sleep, so I'm both, I guess. Why?"

"Just seeing what my odds are if I text you later, whether or not you'll respond."

She giggled. "I guess you'll have to take a chance and find out."

Thane leaned down and kissed her cheek. "I will definitely do that."

"I should go."

"I'll walk you out."

"You don't need to do that, Thane," she said. "You have a crowd of people wanting your attention."

"And they can wait."

She sighed, her heart racing as he laid his hand on her lower back and guided her to her family. Thane shook her uncle's hand. "Thank you for letting me steal her this evening."

Uncle Cary chuckled. "It was all up to her."

Sydney stared at her uncle. He'd just told her it wasn't up to her and that she was being protected whether she wanted to be or not. Now, this man waltzes in, and he's ready to hand her off to him without any information? Not that she minded, but she still found it strange.

Thane kissed Lucy and Aunt Clara's cheeks and then shook Anson's hand before pulling Sydney in for a gentle hug and kissing her cheek again. "I'll text you later."

"Maybe I'll respond," she retorted.

He released her with a chuckle and Sydney walked with her family to the waiting limo.

CHAPTER FIVE

ONCE INSIDE THE car, the barrage of questions began.

"How did you meet Thane Allen?" her aunt asked, her tone excited and fluttery again. "Goodness, he's just as gorgeous in person as he is on screen."

Sydney secured her seat belt. "I accidentally got sent to the interview room when I was waiting for Lucy at the Ritz."

"They were doing press there for the movie," Lucy added.

"How did you *accidentally* get sent there?" Uncle Cary asked.

"*Dad*," Lucy whined.

"Yeah, Dad," Anson piped in. "I highly doubt anyone was trying to kidnap her."

"Does that happen?" Sydney gasped. "I mean, I know kidnapping happens, but do people generally grab someone randomly from a hotel lobby like that? It's the Ritz, not some seedy motel."

"Tell me everything," her uncle said.

Sydney broke down the events of the day, easy to do since they were burned into her brain, and her uncle seemed to relax.

"Well, please don't do that again," he said. "We have to keep security tight, love."

"So, is there a problem if I go out with Thane tomorrow?" she asked.

"I'll coordinate with him on security and go from there."

Sydney slumped in her seat, once again confused by her uncle's flip-flop. "Why do I feel like I'm suddenly five years old all over again?"

"It's not forever, Sydney," her aunt assured her. "Just until the police finalize your mum's accident report."

She sighed. "The guy was drunk and drove head-on into her car. I don't understand why it's taking so long."

"I'll ring the police on Monday," Uncle Cary promised. "Maybe they'll have an update."

"Thanks."

Lucy linked her arm with Sydney's and gave her a bolstering smile, but Sydney didn't feel particularly bolstered. She felt frustrated and powerless. She just wanted things settled so she could get on with her life.

Arriving home, she headed to her room and changed for bed, grateful her family left her alone for the most part. Lucy came in to say good night, but left quickly. Sydney tried to sleep but her mind was on overdrive.

Just when she thought she might need to resort to one of her sleeping pills, her phone buzzed on the nightstand. She grabbed it and smiled down at the screen.

Are you awake, beautiful?

Thane's message was incredibly sweet and Sydney bit her lip, debating on how to respond. She decided to try for funny.

I'm sorry, who is this? I hope you're not a stalker who lurks in movie theaters

I only lurk when the stalkee is trying to avoid me by hiding in the loo

You got me, darn you. But I'm not accustomed to big movie stars stalking me

I should bloody well hope not

Before she could respond, the phone rang and Thane was calling her. She took a deep breath and answered, closing her eyes as his voice floated over the line. "Hi."

"Hi," she whispered. "Shouldn't you be in bed?"

He chuckled. "Who says I'm not?"

Sydney laid her hand on her chest in an effort to calm her heart. The thought of him in bed did something wicked to her. "How much longer did you stay?"

"About an hour after you left and then a few of us went out for a nightcap," he said.

Sydney sank further into her pillows and smiled. "Sounds fun."

"I'd rather have been anywhere else with you, but tomorrow will come, even if it takes forever."

Her stomach fluttered. "About that."

"That sounds ominous."

"I...well, I'm not sure ominous is the right word."

"Are you telling me we can't go out tomorrow?"

"No, it's not that."

"Then what is it, love?" he asked. "Because your uncle and I have already spoken briefly about the security issue."

"You have? When?"

"Just a few minutes ago."

"Oh."

"Tell me, love," he pressed.

"I guess I just don't get why me." She shook her head. "And I'm not saying that in a woe-is-me kind of way. I'm just a little confused. We're so different."

"Because I'm Scottish and you're American?"

"Cute." She giggled. "You're this mega-huge movie star and I'm just some girl from California who has no idea what she's going to do with the rest of her life. I have a degree in communications, but right now, I have no desire to communicate anything to anyone."

He chuckled. "Well, that might all be true, *technically*, but it doesn't change who we are on the inside, and I'd love to get to know you."

"I guess I can't argue with that."

"No, you can't. So, what time am I picking you up tomorrow?"

"I think I should meet you." Sydney picked at a feather making its way out of her comforter. "My uncle will insist on one of his guys driving me."

"Like I said, we already discussed it. I have sent him my men's dossiers and he's doing a further check, but barring any issues, it's already settled."

Sydney chewed her bottom lip. "Okay, that works."

"What are you worried about, love?"

"You think I'm worried?"

"Aye, lass, I do."

"I guess I am, but how would you know that?" she whispered.

"I can feel it." He sighed. "We'll talk more tomorrow, but you can trust me, Sydney. If you need me, I'm here."

"But I don't know you."

"Do you trust me?"

"Am I stupid if I do?"

"Do you think you're stupid?" he challenged. "I don't mean to double-talk you, but have you ever been a bad judge of character?"

"I'm not sure I've been alive long enough to know that definitively, but I'm typically pretty good at figuring out who isn't honest. I get a vibe, I guess you could say."

"And do you get a vibe with me?" he asked. "A bad one, I mean."

"Honestly, no. But it's easier to say that over the phone."

"How do you mean?"

She picked at the feather again. "It's dumb."

"Tell me."

"It's just that when you touch me, I'm totally calm. I feel like myself and don't feel nervous or like we're different. I feel completely in sync with you. Almost like we're meant to be together." She groaned. "Oh my word, I can't believe I just said that out loud. I don't mean we're meant to be together in—"

"Sweetheart, it's all right," he interrupted with a chuckle. "I feel the same way."

"You do?"

"Aye, lass, I do."

"Oh, good." She smiled. "So, you're just as crazy as me, then."

"No doubt in my mind."

Sydney forced back a yawn somewhat unsuccessfully. "Sorry."

"You should sleep, love."

"I don't really want to."

"But you should all the same. I'll ring your uncle tomorrow and we'll get a game plan for security, okay?"

"Sounds good." She suddenly felt a little sad that they were ending their phone call.

"Hey."

"Hmm?" she whispered.

"Can't wait for tomorrow."

"Me neither."

"Sleep, love."

Sydney grinned. "I'll try."

"I'll ring you tomorrow."

"Okay. 'Bye."

"'Bye, love."

He hung up and Sydney snuggled under the covers, falling asleep almost immediately.

* * *

"So, how did a nice American girl end up in rainy old England?" Thane asked, after they'd been seated by the hostess.

Sydney smiled wistfully. Such an innocent question with so many complicated layers of emotion.

After Thane's conversation with Uncle Cary, her uncle had given the green light for him to pick her up. Apparently, he was comfortable with Thane's legion of bodyguards.

"Sorry, love. I didn't mean to bring up something difficult."

Sydney shook her head. "No, it's fine. I guess I just haven't had to tell anyone the story before." She sighed. "I'm actually British. I was born here. Dad was American, though, and he had this brilliant opportunity to move to California to work for a tiny little company called Monarch."

She knew Thane would have heard of Monarch—it had been acquired by the largest social media company in the world.

Thane let out a quiet whistle. "Wow, really?"

Sydney nodded. "He was employee number seven. And, yes, he made a stupid amount of money... not that it saved him."

Thane laid his hand over hers, calming her.

She blinked back tears. "He died six years ago of lung cancer."

"I'm so sorry, love."

She gave him a sad smile. "Non-smoker, tragic story, pretty much sucked. Mom did her best to keep life going. I was still in college, so she decided not to move back here." When Thane released her hand to reach for his handkerchief, she felt the heart-wrenching pain come fast and hard. "I'm sorry. I need a minute."

Standing, she walked as quickly as she could without running, past the hostess desk and into the cold of early evening. Her cheeks froze almost immediately and she realized she was crying. She hadn't cried since her mother died... at least, not in the sense of mourning her. Watching sappy movies and crying at Hallmark commercials didn't count, in her opinion. The warmth of a coat settled over her shoulders and she wiped her cheeks quickly. "Sorry."

"Don't be sorry, love," Thane said, and turned her face him. "We can go if you like."

Sydney shook her head and blushed. "I feel like an idiot."

"Why?"

She shrugged. "Because it's our first date and I'm crying. I didn't even cry when my mom died."

"Shite, lass. Yer mum died too?" He frowned. "When?"

"One month, three days, and"—she checked her watch—"six hours ago, West Coast time."

He pulled her into his arms and held her close. "How?"

"Drunk driver," she rasped. "She was almost home and the guy crossed into her lane and hit her head-on. She was dead on impact." She let out a sad chuckle. "I'm an orphan at twenty-four years old. How pathetic is that?"

"Och, sweetheart, it's not pathetic at all."

She closed her eyes and wrapped her arms around his waist. He was so incredibly warm, and not just in temperature. He made her feel instantly at ease, like she'd come home. "She wanted to come back here right after Dad died, but she refused to leave me. It's so stupid. I could have finished school anywhere, or lived in the dorm and finished there. I didn't need her to stay, but we were so close and she wanted to give me time to grow up a bit. I should have made her come back. I shouldn't have let her—"

"Shhh. If your mum was anything like you, I doubt you could have made her do anything, sweetheart."

"But it's my fault she died," Sydney sobbed. She'd never said those words out loud before, but she'd felt them deeper than anyone could have guessed.

"It's not," Thane whispered.

"It feels like it is," she whispered.

"I know."

He stood and held her in the middle of the sidewalk in front of the busy restaurant. She didn't know how long they stood there, but it was long enough to stop the incessant hiccupping that came with crying jags.

He lifted her face and wiped the tears from her cheeks. "It's not your fault," he stressed.

"I know that logically, but sometimes... I guess I just forget."

"Happens to the best of us, love." Thane smiled. "Do you want to go?"

"Not unless you want to." She licked her lips "I'm actually starving. I want a steak as big as my head and at least one bottle of wine."

He laughed. "Right, come on then."

She took his hand and let him lead her back into the restaurant. He held her chair while she sat down and she removed his jacket and laid it across the back of her seat. "Thanks for that."

"Better?" he asked, and sat down.

"Much." Sydney managed a small smile and took his hand. "You know, I really didn't cry."

"When?"

"When Mom died. I did after Dad, but then the tears just kind of dried up." She shook her head. "It's silly."

He gave her hand a gentle squeeze. "It's not silly, sweetheart."

"I guess what I'm trying to say is, thank you."

"Thank you for driving you to tears?"

"Yes, exactly." She grinned. "I quite like you, Thane Allen."

"I quite like you as well, Sydney Warren."

The waiter stopped by and took their order, returning quickly with the wine. He poured it into their glasses and then left them.

"How long are you staying with your aunt and uncle? I take it with different last names, he's your mum's brother?"

Sydney nodded. "I'll be staying with them until I figure out what to do, I suppose. Uncle Cary saved me in so many ways, so I'm in no rush to leave his protective bubble."

"How did he save you?"

"I was so confused after Mom died. I still am, I guess. But I was also just kind of numb. They flew over immediately and went into 'solve Sydney's life problems' mode." She grimaced. "They took care of the memorial service, cremation details, helped with the will and financial planning. My uncle organized everything and put it together on this lovely little flash drive that I can access anytime I need to. Lucy had been bugging me for years to come and live with them and doubled the effort after Mom's death, so I did."

"But?"

"*But*, I'm not used to the heightened security and the cloak and dagger stuff that comes with it. Uncle Cary says he wants security with me until the final police report comes back on Mom's death, but he hasn't really given me a reason why. Am I in danger? I'm shocked he let me go out with you tonight."

Thane smiled and squeezed her hand. "Your uncle trusts that I will keep you safe, and my job is to make sure you have so much fun, you forget that you have security following you. I take my job very seriously."

Sydney giggled. "I'm picking up on that."

"Will you let me distract you?"

"Don't you have a home or job to go to?"

"I'm done with the promo tour for the movie and I haven't committed to anything new, so I'm at your disposal for as long as you'll have me."

"What if it's forever?"

He leaned forward and winked. "Then I'm at your disposal forever."

She shivered and smiled. What a beautiful prospect.

"Excuse me?" a feminine voice asked.

Sydney glanced up at two teenage girls giggling and blushing as they stared at Thane. "Can we get a photo, please?"

"Do you mind, sweetheart?" he asked Sydney.

"Not at all," she said. "Go right ahead."

Thane took a few minutes to sign autographs and take photos, but his agreeing to do so for the girls meant they were inundated with requests from other diners.

Just when Sydney thought they'd never get the chance to eat, the restaurant manager shooed the fans away and ushered her and Thane into a private room overlooking the Thames.

"Thank you," Thane said, and sat down after Sydney. "We probably should have done this at the beginning."

"It's okay," Sydney said. "I know you were trying to make me feel comfortable by keeping me in a public place."

He chuckled. "I suppose that's true. I'm trying to shake my stalker reputation."

"I thought *I* was the stalker."

"I guess that's closer to the truth, eh?"

The sound of Fallen Crown's single for the new movie piped in and Thane shook his head. "Do you think they did that on purpose?" he mused.

Sydney giggled. "I think it's a big possibility. It's a great song."

"Aye, love, 'tis." He rose to his feet and held out his hand. "Dance with me."

"Here?"

"Why not? We're alone. No one will see us."

She settled her hand in his. "So, twerking is on the table, then?"

"You can twerk on a table?"

"Honey, I can twerk upside down if required."

Thane let out a roar of laughter as he pulled her to her feet. "Bloody hell, sweetheart, you're funny."

Sydney grinned and slid into his arms. He held her close and danced her around the room as the music played quietly.

Þú verður að vera min að eilífu.

"What does that mean?" she asked, a shiver sliding down her spine.

He leaned back slightly and smiled. "You will be mine forever."

"You're so sure of that, huh?"

Thane pulled her close again and kissed her hair. "Hopeful."

"You need to stop being sweet, Thane. You'll ruin your reputation."

He chuckled. "It'll be our secret."

"What language was that?"

"Icelandic."

"You speak Icelandic?"

"A little," he said. "It's part of my heritage."

"Wow, that's really cool." She wove her fingers into his hair and stroked his neck. "Our heritage is all of the English-speaking variety. I wish I spoke another language."

"Stick with me, baby, and I'll translate the world for you."

"Would that be the whole world, or just the world as I know it?"

"Whatever you want, Sydney. I'll make it happen."

"Big words, mister movie star."

He chuckled. "Aye, lass, but true all the same."

She closed her eyes, letting him hold her as they swayed gently to the music.

"Do you know how beautiful you are?" he whispered.

She smiled up at him. "Back atya."

He stared at her for several seconds before leaning forward with a grin. As his lips covered hers, she gripped his waist, opening her mouth. She sighed as he stroked her neck and deepened the kiss. To say he rocked her world was an understatement.

The clearing of a throat and then a voice saying, "I apologize," interrupted them.

Thane broke their connection but kept an arm around her waist. "No worries," he said, and guided Sydney back to the table.

Even though her stomach rumbled, she was disappointed their moment was broken. She wanted to keep dancing and kissing...but mostly kissing. Good Lord, he could kiss.

They didn't speak as the server set their food in front of them, but Thane kept hold of her hand and ran his thumb gently over her knuckles.

"Is there anything else I can get you?" the server asked.

"No. This is great," Thane said. "Thank you."

"Very good, sir." He turned and walked out the door.

Thane stood with a grin. "Before we eat...one more kiss."

Sydney raised her head and Thane kissed her gently. "You're really good at that," she said.

He chuckled and took his seat again. "Back atya."

"So, what's your story?" she asked as they ate.

"That's one I'd rather wait to tell you."

"Oh? How come?"

"Because it's long and in-depth and somewhat hard to believe."

"Well, now I'm even more intrigued."

He smiled. "Let's get to know each other better, love, and I'll tell you everything you need to know."

"Wait." She frowned. "Are you a criminal?"

"No," he stressed. "Nothing nefarious, sweetheart."

"Are you sure?"

"Aye, love, I'm sure." He smiled. "What did your uncle find?"

"What do you mean?"

"When he did the background check."

She cocked her head. "How did you know about his background check?"

"I didn't until you just told me."

Sydney gasped. "Seriously? Crap. I need to be better about that."

"Honestly, I figured he'd do one. I would."

She sipped her wine. "He didn't find anything."

He smiled.

"But you knew that already, didn't you?" she challenged.

"Yes. He wouldn't have been so agreeable if he'd found anything."

Sydney sighed. "I don't know if I'll ever get used to all this cloak and dagger stuff."

"I suppose it would feel a bit like that." He squeezed her hand. "But you understand it's a safety issue, right?"

"I get why *you'd* need security... women wanting to rip your clothes off and everything... but I'm just a girl from California who has no enemies...or admirers." She grimaced. "At least, I don't think I do."

"I'm sure you don't," he agreed. "But this is something you're going to have to get used to, especially being with me."

"I have to get used to it," she said rather than asked.

"Aye."

"Which means you think we'll be together long enough for me *to* get used to it."

Thane grinned. "Aye, lass, I do."

She shook her head. "You're really intense."

"Am I?" he asked, but he was still grinning.

"You know you are."

"Am I frightening you?"

"Honestly?" Sydney rolled her eyes. "No. Which is weird, but I feel a connection to you that seems to defy logic."

"Aye, lass, it does."

She narrowed her eyes. "And you know why."

Thane grinned. "Aye, lass, I do."

"Are you going to explain?"

He nodded. "But not here."

"Hmm, that sounds very mysterious. Are you an international spy?"

"Shhh, keep your voice down," he whispered, a cheeky grin on his face. "They'll find me."

Sydney giggled. "We wouldn't want that."

"No, no, we wouldn't." He linked his fingers with hers. "I'll explain everything in time. Do you trust me?"

"Yes." She squeezed his hand. "As strange as that is, I do."

"It's not strange."

"Crap!" she whispered when she caught sight of her watch. "I'm afraid I have to get home. I am Cinderella after all."

"Right," Thane said. "Sorry, love."

"No, it's okay. I appreciate you humoring my uncle, even if I feel like a teen on prom night. I hate having a curfew."

"It won't be forever." Thane stood and helped Sydney with her jacket. He smiled and leaned down for a quick kiss. "Tomorrow I'll take you up in the Eye."

"No."

"No?"

"Terrified of heights," she admitted. "I'm happy to skip that attraction."

He chuckled. "No problem. We'll find something else to do."

"Lucy wants me to meet her new man. Want to double?"

"That might work. We'll talk about it tomorrow."

Sydney nodded and followed him out of the restaurant. They were met by paparazzi and fans, but Thane made quick work of getting into the waiting car, and then they were off. The driver pulled up to her home twenty minutes later and Thane walked her to the door.

"I hate that we're cutting this short, but if you need me, call me."

She giggled. "I think I can survive a night without hearing your voice."

"Okay, maybe I'll call you, then."

"Silly man." Sydney kissed him gently. "I'll see you tomorrow."

Thane nodded and Sydney let herself inside, locking the door behind her. She waved out the side window and Thane headed to the car. As soon as he was inside, she climbed the stairs to her bedroom and flopped onto the bed. She was in love. As stupid as that sounded, it was true. She was in trouble.

CHAPTER SIX

S*YDNEY?*

Sydney sat straight up, a chill running down her spine. "What?"

She'd been teetering on the edge of wakefulness and sleep, so close to falling over the side and passing out, but then she heard a voice.

Were you sleeping?

She squeaked and sat up on her knees. "Hello?"

Don't be frightened, lass.

"I'm hearing voices and you're telling me not to be frightened?"

Technically, it's just one voice.

"Oh my word," she breathed. "Who are you? No, don't answer that. Holy crap, I'm talking to myself."

A masculine chuckle sounded in her mind. *No, love, you're talking to* me.

Sydney closed her eyes and took several deep breaths. *Please don't kill me, freaky Jason.*
I quite liked that movie.
Thane?
Aye, lass.
"Stop," she hissed. "Just stop."
"Sid? You okay?" Lucy called, and knocked.
"Yeah, sorry. Must have had a bad dream."
Lucy pushed open the door. "Mum and Dad just got home. Do you want to join us for a movie?"
"I'm actually really tired. Rain check?"
"Of course." Lucy smiled. "Good night."
"'Night," Sydney said, and flopped back onto the pillows as Lucy pulled the door closed.
I didn't mean to frighten you, love.
Says the man who keeps talking to me in my head!
Well, now that you've got the hang of it...
Oh, stop!
Close your eyes, he said.
She reached for her cell phone and dialed his number.
He picked up immediately. "Hi."
"How are you doing that?" she demanded.
"It's part of my heritage, I guess you could say."
"What kind of heritage allows you to speak telepathically?" she whispered.
"That'll take a little longer to explain."
Sydney sighed. "This is impossible."
"I know, love." *Now, close your eyes.*
No. Even as she thought her denial, she did as he requested. She wasn't afraid anymore.
Are your eyes closed?
She smiled. *Nope.*
Take a deep breath.
Why?
Just do it.
She wrinkled her nose. *Bossy.*
Aye, lass, I can be. Now, take a deep breath.

Sydney drew air deep into her lungs.
Let it go.
She let out a quiet groan as she did. *Now I'm going to have that song stuck in my head.*
Sorry, love.
Why do I feel the need to build a snowman now?
Sounds like fun.
She smiled. *It does, doesn't it? I never got to experience snow unless I drove for hours to find it.* Her heart started to race, but within seconds she was calm again. "You're doing that, aren't you?" she asked out loud, still connected to his call.
"Aye, lass. I'm going to hang up, but you can call me back if this is overwhelming, okay?"
"Ah...okay." She lowered her cell phone after he disconnected.
You okay?
She nodded. *Why? How?*
I'll save the how for when I see you again.
She squeezed her eyes shut. "I'm insane," she whispered, although, she felt perfectly at ease.
You're not, love.
Why am I not freaking out right now?
It's our connection. It's a lot to take in, but I promise you'll understand everything in time.
She grabbed her phone and dialed his number again. "This is a little too crazy," she said when he answered.
Thane chuckled. "I understand. Thanks for trying."
"Is this an Icelandic thing?"
"Aye. We are an ancient people who have a few abilities that surpass humans."
She gasped. "Are you saying you're not human?" she whispered frantically.
"I'm not going to have this conversation with you until we're face to face. I don't want you freaking out on me."
"It's a little late for that, Thane."
He sighed. "Just give me until tomorrow."
"You keep asking for time, Thane, but you're only giving me partial information. I feel like I'm trapped in a bizarre vampire no-

vel, and let me tell you something, buddy, just because you tell me something's true doesn't mean I'm going to believe you." She squeezed her eyes shut.

"I'm sorry, sweetheart, I know this is frustrating, but my hands are a wee bit tied since all my proof's at home."

"Well then, you may want to figure out a way to untie them, because I don't feel comfortable moving forward with this relationship until you can provide me with cold hard facts. None of this makes any sense."

"Are you saying you won't see me until that happens?"

"Why do you sound surprised?" She frowned.

"Because I am," he snapped.

"Don't get irritated with me, Thane Allen. You're the one trying to tell me you're a vampire."

"I'm not a bloody vampire, Sydney."

She rubbed her forehead. "Are you immortal?"

"How did you get to immortal?" he challenged. "I said I had abilities. I said nothing about immortality."

"I don't know, honestly." She blinked back frustrated tears. "It just came to mind. Are you?"

"Immortal, no, but I do live much longer than humans."

"You're crazy!"

"I don't want to fight with you, sweetheart." He let out a long breath. "Especially when we can't make up properly and in person."

"I don't want to fight either, but you're kind of driving me nuts."

"Come home with me."

"Excuse me?"

"This weekend," he said. "Come home with me. I'll talk to your uncle and figure out the logistics, but if you do, I can show you everything."

"Where is home?" she asked.

"Edinburgh."

"Alone with you?" she clarified. "I'm not that kind of girl, Thane." She couldn't keep the smile from her face at her jab.

"I know that, love. You can stay with Niall and Charlotte if you feel more comfortable. They live very close to me."

She forced down her excitement at the prospect. A whole weekend with him, without the prying eyes of her uncle's security was enticing. Not to mention, fangirls nowhere near them.

"Sydney?" he pressed.

"I've never been to Edinburgh."

"You did that on purpose." He chuckled. "Making me think you were weighing the options."

She grinned, her irritation quickly forgotten. "Maybe."

"I'll work out the details with your uncle and we'll talk tomorrow, okay?"

"Okay." Sydney flopped back onto her pillows. "How will we get there?"

"I typically fly—"

"So you *are* a vampire, then?"

"Only on Sundays."

Sydney giggled. "That's an option?"

"If you twerking on a table is an option, then why wouldn't being a vampire on Sunday be one?"

"You have a point," she conceded.

He chuckled. "If you don't want me to don my cape and fly you to Edinburgh, there is always the option to take the train."

"Oh," she breathed out. "The train sounds amazing."

"I can have Pam look into it."

She smiled. "Do you mind?"

"Why would I mind? The train's a lovely way to get there."

"Are you always this agreeable?"

He chuckled again. "Absolutely."

"Liar."

"I'll let you go back to sleep, sweetheart and we'll talk tomorrow."

She yawned. "Okay."

"Sleep, baby."

She yawned again. "Okay."

"'Bye," he whispered.

"'Bye." She hung up and stared at the ceiling for longer than she would have liked before sleep took her.

* * *

The next morning, Lucy burst into her room and bounced up and down on the mattress. "You're going to Scotland."

"Hmm?" Sydney mumbled.

"Get up."

"Huh? Why are you waking me, evil one?"

"It's almost six," Lucy said.

"In the morning?" Sydney squeaked. She'd slept for almost five hours, a record for her.

"Yep." Lucy bounced again. "And Dad said you're going to Scotland with Thane. Ohmigod, Sid. Thane Allen is whisking you away to his lair."

Sydney pulled the covers over her head. "Go away. I want more sleep."

Lucy yanked the duvet from her face. "Wake up, wake up, wake up. We have to pack."

"Why do we have to pack now?"

"Because the train leaves at like eight. Thane said he'll be here to pick you up at seven."

"Then you go with him," she argued, and rolled away from her cousin.

Lucy smacked her butt. "I'm going to pack sexy undies and nothing else if you don't get out of this bed."

"Wait." Sydney sat up, her hair falling in front of her face. She found the scrunchy that fell out during the night and pulled her hair into a ponytail. "Start again, Luce, and talk really slowly."

Lucy giggled. "Thane is taking you to Edinburgh, and the train leaves at eight. He'll be here at seven to collect you."

"But he said he'd call me today to talk about it."

"Well, he talked to Dad and is now on his way."

"Uncle Cary said that was okay?"

"Yep." Lucy walked into Sydney's closet, returning with a suitcase. "Go shower and then we'll pack."

Sydney jumped from the bed with a squeal and rushed into the bathroom, taking the fastest shower in history. Dressing in dark jeans, black knee-high boots, and a cowl-necked cream sweater, she left her hair in a ponytail, rather than washing it. It would take too long to dry.

"You look gorgeous," Lucy said.

Sydney giggled. "Thanks, cuz. Okay, let's figure out what I'm taking."

"Shoes. You need shoes."

"I need sneakers and flats, maybe slippers."

"No, you need one-, two-, *and* four-inch heels, plus sneakers, flats, and definitely slippers...oh, and boots."

"I'm going for the weekend," Sydney argued. "Not a month."

"At least take your Jimmy Choos and a little black dress. In case."

"Fine." Sydney rolled her eyes. "Just in case."

Lucy helped her pack the rest of her things, which meant Lucy threw stuff into the bag while Sydney took half of it back out. If she hadn't, she'd have needed more than one bag and they would have been packing for a week.

A knock at the door brought her aunt. "Thane's here, love."

Sydney checked her watch. "He's early."

Aunt Clara chuckled. "He obviously wants to get the romance started."

"Oh, gross, Mum," Lucy complained.

"Why is that gross?"

"Probably because you said it."

Sydney grinned and pulled her bag off the bed. "I'm ready. You two can bicker on your own time. Right now, it's romance time."

Aunt Clara giggled and Lucy groaned.

"Just FYI, it's gross when you say it too, Sid," Lucy retorted.

"At least I'm not saying lover."

"Ohmigod, that's disgusting."

Sydney wrinkled her nose. "I'm going away with my loverrrrr."

"Okay, even I think that's gross," Aunt Clara said.

"Which he's not," Sydney rushed to say. "Just to be clear."

"We know," Aunt Clara said, and the three dissolved into giggles as they walked downstairs.

Sydney set her bag in the foyer and smiled when Thane and her uncle walked out of the parlor.

Thane leaned down to kiss her gently. "Good morning. You look beautiful."

"So do you," she said.

He wore dark jeans with a periwinkle-blue sweater that matched his eyes, and to say he looked gorgeous was an understatement.

"Are you ready?"

Sydney nodded. "I tried to pack light."

Thane chuckled. "You did well, love. I was expecting triple."

"I can go back upstairs and pack more if you need me to," she retorted.

He grinned. "Cheeky."

Thane nodded to his "man" who stood inside the door, and he took Sydney's bag out to the car. Sydney took a few minutes to hug her family and then Thane ushered her out to the waiting SUV. The driver held the door open for her and she climbed in while Thane walked to the other side. His phone pealed and he took the call as the driver pulled away from the curb.

"Morning, Pam. Aye." He took Sydney's hand and linked his fingers with hers. "Aye. You did? Well done. Aye. See you in a few minutes." He hung up and smiled. "Pam's diverted the paparazzi, which means, if all goes according to plan, we won't be bothered at the station."

"I didn't even think about the paparazzi," Sydney admitted.

Thane kissed her palm. "That's why we have Pam."

Sydney giggled. "I'm not sure I'm her favorite person."

"Why do you say that?"

"Because I keep distracting you from what *she* wants you to do."

Thane chuckled. "Pam's protective, but she knows who signs her checks, so you won't have any issues with her. If you do, tell me."

"I'm not getting between you and your assistant, Thane. I'll fight my own battles if I need to."

"Sassy."

"Bossy."

He dropped his head back and laughed. "You're gorgeous, you know that, right?"

"Back atya."

He leaned over and kissed her quickly, smiling against her lips. "I can't wait to spend the entire weekend with you."

"Me neither." She cocked her head. "Uncle Cary discussed me staying with you instead of Charlotte and Niall, right?"

"Aye, he did."

"Is that still okay?"

He chuckled. "Of course it is. It's better. We'll have no distractions."

"Perfect," she said. The SUV pulled up to the train station and Thane guided her directly to their private train car.

"Shouldn't we check in?" she asked.

"My people will do that for us." He pulled her to a seat next to the window and sat down beside her.

"So this is what it's like to travel with a big movie star," she mused.

Thane chuckled. "Do you find it to be a positive or a negative?"

"Being whisked into a private rail car? Positive," she said. "Being accosted by sixteen-year-olds with barely any clothes on? Negative."

He grinned. "I'll keep that in mind."

A young man in uniform made his way to them and smiled. "Sir, ma'am, may I get you a drink or something to eat?"

"Coffee," Sydney said immediately. "Please."

"Same," Thane said. "What would you like for breakfast?"

"Surprise me." Sydney grinned. "But definitely something with bacon."

Thane chuckled. "Everything's better with bacon."

"A valuable motto to live by."

Thane focused back on the server. "Full breakfast, please."

"Very good, sir."

The server walked away and Sydney leaned against Thane. He slid his arm around her waist and pulled her closer.

"Careful, honey, I'll fall asleep if you make me any more comfortable," Sydney warned, settling against his chest.

He chuckled. "Sleep, baby. We've got time."

"But there's bacon coming," she whispered even as her eyes were closing.

"I'll wake you when it gets here," he promised.

She nodded with a smile and snuggled closer. She didn't even remember falling asleep, but as promised, Thane woke her to eat. Even with the lure of bacon, she was hard-pressed to leave the comfort of his arms, but the pig won out and she devoured her meal.

CHAPTER SEVEN

"Wow," Sydney exclaimed with a low whistle as they drove through wrought-iron gates and down a long drive. "All of this is yours?"

"Aye, love."

The train ride had been breathtaking. Well, it had been breathtaking for as long as she'd managed to stay awake, but a full belly and strong arms to hold her had her falling asleep shortly after breakfast. Thane had awakened her right before they pulled into the station, so she only got a brief look at the passing scenery and then they were pulling into the depot.

Thane's home came into view and it was like something out of a medieval movie, the white stone house that looked more like a mansion sitting on acreage that rivaled a king's fiefdom.

"It's a Scots Baronial property," he said. "I built it in 1760 and refurbished it a few years ago."

"*You* built it?"

"Aye, lass."

"Just how old *are* you?" she whispered.

He smiled. "Two hundred and eighty-five."

"Shut up."

Thane chuckled. "I know it's a lot to take in."

"Ya think?"

The car pulled up to the front door and Thane took Sydney's hand, leading her inside. "I have about a hundred-twenty-five acres which we can explore this weekend. I'm not sure if you ride, but I have horses and we can take them out whenever you like."

Sydney nodded as she took in the space. "I love horses."

Thane's home had five bedrooms, four bathrooms, something he called a reception hall, but it was more of a room with historic furniture inside, drawing room, kitchen, family room, library... she kind of zoned out as he kept listing rooms. She knew it would take some time to explore the entire house, not to mention the property.

There was apparently a cottage somewhere as well, with two bedrooms, two bathrooms, and all the necessities of a separate home.

"Sweetheart?"

"Hmm?" Thane squeezed her hand and she came back to the present. "Oh, sorry. I'm trying to take it all in. What did I miss?"

He grinned. "Nothing, love. Come on, I'll show you to your room."

"I'm going to get lost," she said as he led her upstairs.

"No you won't. If you do, just let me know." He tapped his temple.

"Or, you could just stay glued to my side at all times."

"That works too." He pushed open a large mahogany door and stepped back for her to precede him inside.

A king-sized wrought-iron bed sat to the right as she walked into the room, a fireplace was centered on the wall opposite the bed, and two high-backed chairs created a reading area facing a large picture window overlooking the grounds. She could see the cottage and a large white barn off in the distance.

"Thane, this is incredible," she said, and smiled over at him.

"I'm glad you like it. You have your own bathroom and a closet through that door there." He pointed to the door next to the fireplace. "I'm right next door, so I'm close if you need me in the middle of the night."

She wrapped her arms around his waist. "You'll scare away my bad dreams?"

"You have bad dreams?"

"Not often, to be honest." She glanced up at him. "I don't typically sleep much."

He tugged gently on her ponytail. "I will scare away anything that might frighten you."

Sydney giggled. "My true knight in shining armor."

"Always." He smiled, leaning down to kiss her.

As he deepened the kiss, a flash of light then a loud boom of thunder sounded, and Sydney broke their connection with a grin. "Wow, you rocked my world, honey. Literally."

"Just wait," he promised, and walked to the window just as rain pelted the glass. "So much for exploring."

"I'm up for cozy make-out time with wine as well, you know. Especially if it involves answers to all these weird questions... oh, and more world rocking."

He faced her and crossed his arms. "The answers could take all night."

She shrugged. "I'm okay with that."

Thane held out his hand and Sydney took it, following him downstairs and into the library. And it was *literally* a library. The room was larger than most master bedrooms and had bookshelves that covered three of the four walls, all loaded with a majority of hardback books. The dark mahogany wood and overstuffed furniture, perfect to relax and read on, made her feel like Hemingway would have loved it here. She did too. It was gorgeous.

Thane released her and pushed open a bookshelf to reveal a private room.

"Oh my word, you have a Scooby Doo room!"

Thane chuckled and waved her to follow. "This I added in the 1800s when I redesigned the library."

"It's so cool." Sydney stepped inside. This room was a third the size of the library and somewhat bare. A couple of bookshelves held books that looked a lot older than Thane, and there was a large table in the middle covered with papers. It appeared to be a research room of some sort.

He pulled a heavy book off a shelf and set it in the middle of the table. "This is my family history as far back as we began recording such things."

Sydney ran her fingers over the soft leather. "Wow, it's beautiful."

"It's mostly written in Icelandic," he said, and opened the book to about two-thirds in. "But here is where my entries begin in English."

Sydney flipped back a little bit and pointed to a number. "What does this say?"

"This talks of when my parents immigrated to Scotland with the king's family in 1420."

"Your parents did?"

"Aye, lass."

"Are they still alive?"

He nodded.

"Seriously?" Her mouth gaped open.

"Aye. They live not far from here."

"Are you close?"

"Very."

She bit her lip. "Do they know about me?"

Thane chuckled. "Aye, lass, they do. They attempted to finagle a dinner out of me for this weekend, but I put them off."

"You don't need to do that on my account."

"I wanted to give you time to understand everything."

Sydney smiled. "Well, you better get to explaining. I want to meet the people who made you."

He grinned and kissed her quickly. "Okay. I will give you the bullet points that pertain to us specifically and you can ask questions as they arise. Sound good?"

"Sounds perfect."

"When you walked into the interview room at the hotel, I knew you were my mate."

"Your mate? How?"

"Twenty-five is the *ár mökun*, the mating year. It's when our hearts turn to whoever our mates are, if they're close. So as soon as I reached mating year, I knew I would know you as soon as I saw you."

"Will I know you're my mate when I turn twenty-five?"

"Possibly," he said. "It's different for humans, so you may not. At least not the way we do."

"I guess we'll have to wait a month."

"Your birthday's in a month?"

"Yep." She studied the book again.

He slid his hand to the back of her neck and squeezed gently. "What, love?"

"It'll be my first without my mom."

"Och, sweetheart, it will be. I'm sorry." He pulled her close and she did a face plant into his chest. "We'll just have to make it extra special, eh?"

"I'm not a big group person, so please, no party."

He cupped her face and raised her chin. "No party. I promise."

Leaning down, he kissed her and she wrapped her arms tighter around his waist. He broke their connection far too quickly, and she reluctantly went back to the book.

"So, the mate thing," she prompted.

"Aye. When I touched you in the interview room, our *örlög*... fate, was sealed." He kept an arm around her waist as they skimmed the book. "And when I first spoke to you in your mind, our connection began."

"Do you have to say special words to start the connection?"

"No, but the first thing I said to you was 'Þú verður að vera min að eilífu.' They are some of the first words we speak to our mates."

"But you said that out loud," she countered.

"No, I didn't, actually. You just assumed I did." He smiled. "It's how I knew I found the path to your mind so that I could speak with you later."

"Yeah, 'cause that wasn't creepy," she grumbled.

Thane chuckled.

"So, is there more to this 'mating' thing?" she asked with a blush.

"When you're ready, I'll bind you, and you'll become like me."

She laid a hand on his chest. "Whoa, hold up there, skippy. What do you *mean*, I'll become like you?"

"The binding is our version of a wedding ceremony, only it's private. I will bind you spiritually and then when we make love, I will bind you physically. Your body will go through a conversion of sorts and you will become Cauld Ane. You'll take on many, if not all, of my abilities and you will live as long as I do."

"I'll be immortal?"

"Not immortal, no, but you'll live a thousand years or so, very likely."

She let out a deep breath. "Wow."

"It's a lot to take in, love. There's no rush."

"Can you bind me now?"

"No. I can't bind you until you're twenty-five."

She snapped her fingers and retorted, "Shoot."

Thane chuckled.

"So, mating, is it like marriage?"

"It's far more permanent. When mates find one another, even if they aren't bound, they are connected forever."

"So, no cheating or whatever?"

He shook his head. "It's impossible for us."

She leaned into him. "That would be so nice to never have to worry about something like that."

"I suppose so, yes. We've never known any other way, but thinking about the possibility isn't pleasant."

She shuddered. "No, it's not."

"Have you had to deal with that?"

Sydney smiled. "No. I haven't really dated much. I met a couple of guys at church, but with all the stuff going on with my parents, I didn't go back. Crisis of faith maybe."

"It's understandable, love."

"Lucy says I'm a little like my mom... I bury my head in the sand when things get sad."

"We all process things differently, Sydney."

She bit her lip and nodded. "I'm coming out of it, though. Even with my mom's death. I'm trying to understand that sometimes shit just happens and it's not God punishing me. I just have to remember that when I'm really sad."

He turned her to face him and stroked her cheek. "If you forget, I'll remind you."

"I already feel like He's watching out for me."

"You do?"

Sydney smiled through the tears. "He brought me to you."

"Och, sweetheart, you're killing me."

"I am?"

He nodded and leaned down. "I love you," he whispered, and kissed her, gripping her waist and lifting her onto the table. He moved to stand between her legs and cupped the back of her head, deepening the kiss.

Sydney slid her hands up his chest and into his hair. She wasn't sure how long they were there, but he broke the kiss all too soon and dropped his forehead to hers. "A month you say?"

She giggled with a nod. "Way too long."

"Aye, love, 'tis."

"I love you, too, by the way," she said, and looped her arms over his shoulders. "Sounds strange to say it so soon, but I mean it."

"I do too, lass." He ran his hands through her ponytail. "I can't wait to make this permanent."

"Same. Am I meeting your family this weekend?"

"Aye, lass. If you'd like to."

"Aye, I'd like to," she mimicked.

"I'll set it up," he promised. "But tonight, you're all mine. I won't share."

"Wine and snuggling better be on the table."

Thane laughed. "I'm not a monster."

"Good to know."

"Shall we shelve this discussion, or do you have more questions?"

"We can shelve it."

"You can ask me anything you need to and this room is open to you any time you want."

Sydney smiled. "Thank you."

"Come on, let's go find something to eat."

"Mmm, yes, please." She slid off the table and took his hand, following him out of the library and toward the kitchen.

* * *

At almost midnight, after Thane kissed her at her bedroom door, Sydney stepped inside and started to prep for bed. She couldn't help peeking outside at the storm. She'd always loved a good thunder and lightning show, but rarely got them in California.

A shot of lightning hit and she was drawn to a shadow out by the cottage. At first she thought her eyes were playing tricks on her until lightning lit up the sky again. She gasped. A man stood looking right up at her, if that was even possible.

Sydney, you okay?

I think someone's out by the cottage.

I'm coming in.

"Okay," she said distractedly, still staring out the window.

Another flash of light and the man still stood where he was. Thane reached her and wrapped an arm around her waist, leaning forward to see if he could see what she saw. It took a little longer than the last time, but lightning flashed and there was no one there.

"He was just there," she whispered.

Thane gave her a gentle squeeze. "Are you sure you saw someone?"

"Well, no. I guess not. It could have been a shadow from a tree, I suppose." Lightning hit again and there was still no one there. Sydney sighed. "I must be seeing things."

Thane smiled and turned her to face him. She licked her lips at the sight of him in dark pajama pants and black wife-beater. Running her fingers up his muscular arms, she stroked the pulse at his throat.

"Lightning can create all manner of illusions, but my land is secure, love," he promised. "If someone was on it, I'd have been alerted."

She nodded. "It was probably a tree or something."

"Probably." He kissed her nose.

A clap of thunder rattled the windows and she couldn't help but startle.

"Are you afraid of storms?"

"No. Actually, I love them." She smiled up at him. "I just feel a little off-kilter."

"Do you want to sleep with me?" He stroked her cheek. "No monkey business, I promise."

She giggled. "But monkey business is so much fun."

"Aye, I agree, lass."

"I'm okay. Really," she said. "I won't sleep. I never do and I don't want to keep you awake."

"Why don't you sleep?"

"I don't really know. I haven't for years."

"Do you get *any* sleep?"

"Maybe three hours a night." She shrugged. "Anyway, I don't want to keep you up, so I'll just read or something."

"We can watch a movie, love."

"It's way past midnight, honey."

"So?"

"Don't you need to sleep?"

Thane chuckled. "Sweetheart, if I'm with you, I never have to sleep again."

"Is that a Cauld Ane thing?"

"It's a you and me thing."

"Oh, really?"

"I don't want to waste a second of our time together sleeping," he whispered.

She slid her fingers into his hair. "Charmer."

"Wanna make out some more?"

"Does a bear shit in the woods?"

* * *

Thane laughed, leading her out of her room and into the private sitting room right off his bedroom. He loved her sense of humor. He loved everything about her. "If you fall asleep, I'll carry you to bed."

She giggled. "I won't fall asleep."

"What do you want to watch?"

"Nothing I have to think about." Sydney flopped onto the sofa facing the television. "Would it be weird to watch one of yours?"

Thane grinned and pulled open a floor-to-ceiling cabinet two-deep with DVD's. "Yeah, love, it would be weird."

"You don't watch your own movies?"

"I watch the premiere and then, no, I don't watch them again." He ran his fingers over cases and pulled a couple from the shelves.

"But I love your movies."

He grinned at her over his shoulder. "I appreciate that, sweetheart."

"Did you really date all of your costars? Except Charlotte MacMillan, of course. I heard that somewhere."

"No."

"Really?"

"Really." He closed the cabinet and sat next to her, setting the movies on the coffee table. "Want to choose?"

She leaned forward, grabbed the shoot 'em up, and handed it to him. He slid it into the player and sat beside her again, pressing play. She took the remote and hit pause.

"Did you date *any* of them?" she asked.

"Aye, lass, I did."

"Were any of them Cauld Ane?"

He raised an eyebrow. "No."

"How many of them did you sleep with?"

Thane let out a long sigh. "I think it would be better if I don't answer that."

"*All* of them?" she squeaked.

"No. Not all of them."

"Who?"

"I'm not going to tell you that, Sydney."

She gasped. "What? Why not?"

"Because I can feel your irritation."

"So that means you're never going to tell me which ones you slept with?"

"Not '*never*,' but for now, love, aye."

"Fine." She crossed her arms and sank further into the sofa. "Let's just watch the stupid movie."

He nodded and pressed play again... and waited. He didn't have to wait long before she paused the movie again.

"Why not?"

"Because when I tell you about my dating history, you need to be calm," he said. "Right now, you're not."

"I'm calm," she argued. "I'm so calm, I'm like Zen calm."

He chuckled. "Sydney, you are so far from Zen calm, it's not even funny."

"You're so far from Zen calm, it's not even funny," she mimicked in a sing-song voice.

"Shall we watch the movie?"

"Go ahead." She waved her hand toward the DVD player and then went back to her guarded posture. Ten seconds in, she huffed. "So, did you sleep with most of them?"

He paused the movie again and leaned his head in his palm, resting his elbow against the back of the sofa. "No."

"Just tell me."

"No."

"I'm going to bed." She threw the blanket off and rose to her feet. "*My* bed."

Thane watched her leave with a sigh. He should probably give her a few minutes to calm down, but he could feel her frustration. He shut off the television and stood, heading to her room and knocking on the door.

She pulled open the door and threw herself into his arms. "I'm sorry."

He kissed her temple. "Och, lass, it's alright."

"Jealousy isn't really in my nature."

"Jealousy's in everyone's nature, love."

Sydney shuddered.

"What?"

"Something's wrong." She pulled away from him and rushed to the window. "He's there again."

Thane grabbed the phone and dialed Wallace's number. The man answered on the first ring. "Sir?"

"Check the grounds."

"Aye, sir. What am I looking for?"

"Sydney saw someone over by the cottage." Thane watched as Sydney stared out the window. "Text me when you find anything."

"Aye, sir." Wallace hung up and Thane set the phone back on the cradle.

"He's gone again," Sydney said, turning from the window and running her hands up her arms.

Thane could feel her fear, so he pulled her into his arms again and she sagged against him. "You're safe, sweetheart."

"I just don't understand why I don't *feel* safe. There's no reason for it."

"Come on." He took her hand and led her back to his room, locking the door behind them and leading her to the sofa. "You're staying in here tonight."

"Okay," she whispered.

Pulling her up against his chest, he wrapped the blanket around her and kissed her forehead. "I've got you, love."

"Okay," she whispered again, and settled her cheek against his chest.

He felt her relax in stages. "Better?"

She didn't answer him because she was asleep. Thane smiled and turned the volume on super low, holding her close. His phone buzzed on the table next to him and he reached for it. Wallace didn't find anyone, but he did find cigarette butts, which didn't sit well with Thane.

Shite.

"What?" Sydney mumbled.

"Nothing, love. Go back to sleep."

"Tell me."

"Wallace found cigarette butts, but whoever was out there is now gone."

She sat up and frowned. "Crap."

"Aye."

"Should we leave?"

"There's really no safer place, love. We're locked in and the alarm's set." He gave her a gentle squeeze. "Plus, the men have been alerted, so my team is ready."

"Okay."

"Want to watch the movie or go to bed?"

"Bed, I think."

He turned everything off and pulled her from the couch. "You're going to sleep tonight."

"We'll see."

He cupped her cheeks. "Do you want me to make you sleep?"

"Can you do that?"

"I've done it before."

"What?"

Thane smiled. "Think of the last few times I told you to sleep."

She gasped. "I *did* sleep."

"That doesn't surprise me."

"Don't go getting all superior on me, mister movie star. But I will admit, it was unusual for me to sleep six hours."

He chuckled. "Well, tonight we'll try for eight."

"If you can do that, I'll marry you tomorrow." She looped her arms around his neck. "After I wake up, of course."

Thane kissed her and guided her to the bed, where he pulled her into his arms and wrapped the covers around her. "I love you, sweetheart."

She kissed him and smiled against his lips. "I love you, too."

"Sleep now."

It didn't take long for her to succumb to his words and as soon as he felt her relax, he followed her into slumber.

CHAPTER EIGHT

"W*HO IS THIS? Why do you keep calling?" Sydney's mother demanded into the phone. "If you don't stop, I'll call the police."*

"Mom?" Sydney pushed open the office door and her mother set her phone on the desk. "Everything okay?"

"Fine, honeybun, just a prank caller."

"How many times does this prank caller call?"

"I think this is the second time." She slid the phone into her jeans pocket and her hand shook.

Sydney knew she was lying.

"Let's get lunch."

Sydney nodded and forced a smile. *"Sounds good."*

* * *

Sydney sat straight up with a scream. Thane had felt her fear before she'd awakened, so he was quick to wrap his arms around her and calm her. "I'm here, love. You're okay. It was a dream."

"I keep having this recurring nightmare." She burrowed into his chest. "I think Mom was in trouble."

"You do?"

She nodded. "I just can't figure it out. Why would I think that?"

Thane pulled her down on the pillows with him. "I'll talk to your uncle. Maybe he knows something."

"I don't think he'll tell you anything. He's annoyingly tight-lipped right now."

"He'll tell me, love."

Sydney sat up again.

"Where are you going?" he asked.

She patted his chest. "I'm not going to be able to sleep, honey. I'll go read."

He smiled and tugged her back down. "Sleep, baby."

She did.

* * *

Sydney heard water running and forced her eyes open. She didn't want to wake up. She was warm and cozy tucked in the soft sheets of Thane's bed, so she closed her eyes again and snuggled deeper into the mattress.

"Well, good morning, sunshine," Thane said.

"How did you know I was awake?" she asked, not looking at him.

"Because I did."

Sydney smiled and opened her eyes again, biting her lip at the sight of Thane wearing only jeans, one arm raised, using the towel to dry his hair as he grinned at her. He looped the towel around his neck and leaned down to kiss her gently. "Ten hours."

"Hmm?"

"You slept for ten hours."

"Shut up!" She glanced at the clock on the nightstand. "Holy crap, I *did* sleep for ten hours."

Thane chuckled. "How do you feel?"

"Amazing. I'm hard pressed to get out of this bed."

"Then don't."

"Since I know you're going to help me sleep again tonight, I want to know what it feels like to go through a day feeling normal." She stretched as he moved around the room and she couldn't help but watch him. He was so graceful, not to mention sexy.

"The storm's passed," he said, and pulled a T-shirt over his head. "We can ride the property or walk, whatever you like."

She propped up on her elbows. "Is it safe?"

"Aye, lass. Wallace has seen nothing out of the ordinary."

She grinned. "I'd love to ride, then."

"Perfect." He kissed her quickly and then stepped into the bathroom. "My family has requested we join them for dinner tonight if that works for you."

"Sounds great." Sydney threw the covers off and sat up. "I'll change quickly and meet you back here, okay?"

He leaned out of the bathroom and smiled. "That works. We'll eat then go."

Sydney nodded and headed to her bedroom, grabbing a pair of jeans and a long-sleeved T-shirt from the bureau on her way to the bathroom. She was glad Lucy forced her to bring a pair of boots with a low heel. They'd be perfect for riding.

After washing her face and brushing her teeth, she met Thane back at his bedroom and they headed to the kitchen for breakfast. Sydney's excitement couldn't be contained as they walked out to the barn, especially when she met the horse she would ride. A big black Friesian gelding by the name of Julius. They bonded pretty quickly and Sydney instantly fell in love.

"I think I'm stealing him," she said, and Thane laughed.

"You don't have to steal him, love. If you'd like him, he's yours."

"Really?"

"Of course." Thane patted Julius's neck. "I knew you two would get along."

"Can we just stay here forever?" She hugged him. "I'm okay with never going back to London."

"Whatever you want to do, love, I'll make it happen." Thane stroked her cheek. "But I do think I need to speak with your uncle first and sort out what he knows about your parents."

"Then can we escape from the world for a little while?"

"Of course we can, sweetheart." He frowned. "Why so blue?"

"I just feel like the other shoe's going to drop."

Thane smiled. "I've got you, baby. It's all going to be okay."

"Promise?"

"Promise."

She nodded and kissed him. Julius nuzzled Sydney and she giggled. "You're going to make it all okay, too, aren't you, boy?" He swung his head up and down and Sydney shook her head. "I'm officially in love."

"I think he is too," Thane said. "I don't blame him."

"Charmer."

He kissed her quickly again and then reached for his horse. "Let's ride."

The stable hand helped Sydney mount and she gathered the reins and followed Thane away from the barn. He took her to the cottage first, helping her down and tying off the horses before leading her inside.

"Thane, it's lovely."

The little cottage was older than the main house, but had also been recently updated. The two-bedroom, two-bathroom home had a great room, kitchen, plus a den, and Sydney loved it.

Thane led her back out to the horses and they spent another hour exploring the grounds, forced to return to the barn due to another downpour. By the time they arrived back, they were soaked and Sydney was freezing. A couple of the stable hands took the horses and Thane whisked Sydney back to the house. She discovered he'd called ahead and had one of the staff draw a bath for her. She sank into pure bliss, sighing as the warm water covered her body.

I love you so much right now, you have no idea.

Thane chuckled. *I think I have an inkling.*

Thank you for doing this.

My pleasure, love.

Sydney added hot water to the tub and stared out the window that Thane assured her was of the one-way variety, so she could see out, but no one could see in. *What should I wear tonight?*

Whatever you like.
Typical man.
He chuckled again.
I brought a little black dress with me...or is that too dressed up?
That sounds perfect, love.
What are you doing?
Wishing I was in the tub with you.
She bit her lip. *Join me, then.*
One month, love, and I will.
You're really going to make us wait?
It would be dangerous if I didn't.
Sydney frowned. *How so?*
Because I know it would be impossible to make love to you and not bind you, and binding cannot happen before you're twenty-five.
I'd like to go on record to say that I think that's lame.
I don't disagree, but think of the positives.
Being horny all the time is not a positive, Thane.
No, that's true, but getting to know one another without distraction most definitely is.
Sydney rolled her eyes. *Still sucks.*
I know, baby. I have to speak with Wallace.
Is something wrong?
I don't think so. Enjoy your bath.
And he was gone.

Sydney sighed and sank lower in the water. She didn't want to leave the gigantic claw-foot tub and it sounded as though she didn't have to anytime soon. She was both excited and nervous to meet Thane's family, but mostly nervous. She wondered what the family of an immortal superstar was like. She couldn't begin to imagine. She was still trying to figure out how she'd become inseparable from the biggest movie star on the planet.

Your thoughts are adorable, lass.
Sydney rolled her eyes. *Get out of my brain.*
He chuckled. *We leave in two hours.*
I'll be ready.

Don't be nervous. My family will love you.
She sighed. *I hope so.*

* * *

Sydney gripped Thane's hand as Wallace drove them over a drawbridge (yes, a real freakin' drawbridge) and into the courtyard of the tiniest castle Sydney had ever seen. Granted, she wasn't an expert on castles, and tiny was somewhat relative, but this one looked to be a bit smaller than Thane's home, which was just under twelve-thousand square feet. She'd always expected castles to be monstrous in size, able to house entire villages.

Thane chuckled. "Not quite, sweetheart."

She rolled her eyes. "Brain. Out. Now."

"This has been our home since we arrived from Iceland. We all have part of the land and we've all stayed close. My house is at the far south end of the property."

"It's gorgeous," Sydney breathed.

"It's my home away from home, so to speak." Thane squeezed her hand and then got out of the car. She waited for him to open her door and hold his hand out to her before climbing out herself.

He wrapped his arm tightly around her waist and walked her to the front door, but before they could walk in, Sydney was pulled away and into a surprisingly strong hug, considering the girl was tiny. "You're here," the girl exclaimed.

"Sydney, this is my very little, very dramatic, sister, Ainsley."

"I'm not dramatic; I'm just excited to meet your mate."

Sydney giggled. "I'm excited to meet you as well, Ainsley."

"Everyone's in the salon." Ainsley grinned. "Mum didn't want to overwhelm you with all of us descending upon you."

"That was very kind of her," Sydney said. *She sounds thirty, not twelve.*

Thane grinned. *You have no idea.*

His hand settled on her lower back again and they followed Ainsley into the formal room where close to ten people, not including children, milled around, sipping drinks and talking. Sydney reached for Thane's hand and gripped it hard, hoping for a little burst of confidence.

"Thane!" A stunning redheaded woman who appeared to be in her early thirties rushed them, pulling Thane in for a long hug. "Och, my son, I've missed you."

He chuckled. "It's barely been a month, Mum."

Sydney bit back a gasp. His mother didn't look much older than him.

"Still too long for your poor aging mother," she retorted, and faced Sydney. "Sydney, love, welcome. We're so glad to meet you."

"Thank you, Mrs. Allen. It's lovely to meet you as well."

"Och, love, call me Isolde or better yet, Mum, if you feel comfortable with that. Whatever you choose."

Sydney blushed. "Thank you. That's sweet."

"Come and meet everyone else."

Isolde took over the introductions, but Sydney was grateful Thane stayed connected to her. His father was a giant of a man. His name was Domnall, but they all called him Dom or Da for Father. Thane had an older brother and an older sister, Lachlan and Elspie, who were married to Aggie and Marsh respectively. Then there was a younger brother, Thorburn, who was married to Blair. Finally, Ainsley. All but Ainsley were bound, and it made for a very full house.

Sydney didn't think she'd remember all the adult names, let alone the nine kids. She found herself wondering how quickly she could add to the brood, excited about being part of such a large family.

Right away, love.

She narrowed her eyes at Thane and shook her head. *Get out of my brain.*

He chuckled as he led her to a love seat and pulled her down next to him, wrapping an arm around her and pulling her close. "So, what's on the Allen Family radar right now?" Thane asked.

"The little prince turns one next month," Isolde said, sitting next to her husband.

"Has it been a year already?" Thane mused.

"Aye, and we've been invited for the party, which will be a weekend-long affair."

"Who's the little prince?" Sydney asked.

"Our king and queen, Kade and Samantha Gunnach, have a little boy, Liam, and there's a huge party to celebrate at their castle in Inverness," Thane explained. "I'd forgotten all about it, to be honest, but we can go if you'd like to."

"When do we have to let them know by?"

"We've got time," he assured her.

Sydney smiled. "Okay, good."

"You *have* to go," Ainsley begged.

"Ainsley," her mother warned.

"But, Mummy, if Thane doesn't go, then I won't get to ride Max's horses."

Thane chuckled. "Even if I don't go, lass, Niall will still take you to Max's stables. All I have to do is ask him. You know he'll make it happen."

"But they have a baby now and he's busy."

"Ainsley Meredith Allen," Isolde admonished. "This is not about you."

"Sorry," she grumbled, crossing her arms in silent irritation.

"Max breeds Friesians and works closely with Connall Gunnach, who breeds Thoroughbreds, and now Arabians, due to his mate's influence," Thane explained.

"Ainsley, if you love Friesians, why don't you ride your brother's horses?" Sydney asked.

"Because, sweetheart, I am not the lead singer of Fallen Crown," Thane answered before Ainsley could.

Sydney stifled a giggle at Ainsley's look of mortification.

"Alright, enough teasing the baby," Isolde said.

Sydney leaned forward. "I will figure out a way to make sure your brother goes."

Ainsley's face lit up. "You will?"

"Of course. We can't keep you away from the horses. That would be cruel."

Thane reached for Sydney's neck and gave it a gentle squeeze. *Careful, love, you'll create a monster.*

Before more could be said on the subject, Isolde rose to her feet and ushered everyone into the dining room. Conversation came fast and humorously as everyone sat down to eat. The whole night was...well...normal. No one treated Thane like he was anyone special outside of the third child of this large and loving brood.

"When do you have to return to London?" Elspie asked.

"Tomorrow," Sydney said.

"Oh, that's so soon."

"I know. I have a few things to tie up with my mother's estate, so I need to get back."

"We were sorry to hear about your parents, love," Isolde said.

Sydney forced a smile. "Thanks."

Thane linked his fingers with hers under the table and gave her hand a gentle squeeze.

"I love London," Elspie continued. "Perhaps us girls can meet for a girls-only weekend."

"Day," Thane said.

"I'd love it." Sydney grinned.

"One day," Thane reiterated.

Sydney rolled her eyes. "A weekend or a day is fine with me."

"You can have her for a few hours on *one* of the days you come. No more," Thane decreed.

"We're not beneath kidnapping, Thane." She pointed a knife at him. "Remember that."

Sydney giggled. "I'm also not beneath sneaking out when you're not looking."

"Fine." Thane raised his hands in surrender. "But ganging up on the little brother really isn't very nice."

"Bunk beds, Thane," Lachlan countered.

"One time! It was one time!"

"My arse says it was thrice," Lachlan argued.

The table dissolved into laughter and Sydney watched as the group tried to control their giggles.

"Locky has always been a little gullible," Thane said. "When we were kids I invited him to climb up to the top bunk, where I quickly chucked him off."

"And he's gullible because of that?" Sydney challenged.

"No, he's gullible because he let me do it twice more."

Sydney gasped, forcing back a laugh. "That's awful!"

"It's not my fault he was dumb enough to climb up again."

"So, to make it up to Locky, Sydney gets to go shopping with me," Elspie said.

"To make it up to *me*?" Lachlan countered.

"Yes."

"I just don't think I can do without her for more than a few hours," Thane added.

"You'll survive, honey," Sydney said.

Elspie clapped her hands. "It's a date."

"Wait, I haven't agreed," Thane argued.

"Like that makes a difference," Sydney countered. "I'm not your chattel, which means you have no say in the matter."

Ainsley let out a giggle and Elspie reached over and high-fived Sydney. Thane good-naturedly leaned over and kissed Sydney. "Touché, baby."

Sydney smiled at her soon-to-be sister-in-law. "It's a date, Elspie."

"Great. I'll find a time and we'll make it happen."

"I can't wait," Sydney said.

Dinner wrapped up and Thane insisted on taking Sydney home before it got too late. Another storm was approaching and he didn't want Wallace driving the back-roads in total darkness, so after hugs and promises of future get-togethers, Sydney followed him out to the car.

"Your family's amazing," she said as Wallace guided the car over the drawbridge.

"Aye, they are." He smiled. "And, like I said they would, they adored you."

"Yes, honey, you were right." Sydney giggled. "I adored them as well. I can't wait for Elspie's visit."

"I'm going to venture a guess it'll be sooner than later."

"I hope so." She cocked her head. "Has there ever been an instance where a Cauld Ane family doesn't approve of one's mate?"

Thane shrugged. "I'm sure there has been, but can you imagine what kind of a position that would put the couple in? It'd be a bloody shame."

"What would you do?"

"If my family didn't approve of you?"

"Yes."

He shook his head. "Sweetheart."

"What? It was a possibility."

"No it wasn't," he argued. "But if by some far off chance they hadn't approved, then I would have cut ties with them."

Sydney gasped. "You would?"

"Of course I would." He squeezed her leg. "You're everything to me, Sydney. Don't ever doubt that."

She smiled. "I love you."

"I love you too."

Arriving home, Thane left Sydney to change and she sighed in relief to get her shoes off. Just as she slipped out of her dress, her phone rang. It was Lucy. "Well, hello, cuz, how are you?"

"Have you guys been watching the news?"

"Nope." Sydney dropped her watch onto the dresser. "We've been blissfully unaware of the outside world. Why?"

"Ohmigod, Sid, the world is blowing up about you."

"About me? Why?"

"Because you're dating Thane Allen."

Sydney sat on the bed and rubbed her forehead. "Is it bad or good?"

"Watch the news and entertainment shows and decide for yourself, but I'd suggest you get a game plan before you come home, because we've already started getting phone calls."

"Holy cow."

"Yep. Anyway, I have to go. Date night and all that, but I thought you'd want to know."

"Thanks, Luce. Love you."

"Love you too. 'Bye."

Sydney set her phone on the nightstand. *Have you heard about the gossip surrounding us?*

Aye, lass. Pam filled me in yesterday.

Why didn't you tell me?

Because you needed a break. Finish getting changed and we'll talk about it over a glass of wine.

Sydney sighed and took the time to remove her makeup and change into pajamas. This was all she needed, people digging into her life and invading her privacy. Just great.

CHAPTER NINE

SYDNEY PUSHED THE door to Thane's sitting room open and stepped inside. He was on his phone, pacing by the window and he didn't look happy. "Damn it, Pam, why the hell aren't they leaving it alone? I know, but it's not that bloody interesting. Right. Aye. Fine. Yes, we'll talk tomorrow." He let out a long sigh. "'Night." He hung up and faced Sydney.

"That didn't sound good."

"Just a minor nuisance, love." He rubbed the back of his neck. "Nothing for you to worry about."

"Dismissing me like that isn't the way to go here, Thane."

"It's something my people will figure out, Sydney. Just drop it."

"Your people."

"Yes, my people. It's not really something you can do anything about, so just leave it."

She crossed her arms and stamped down her irritation. "I think I should be filled in, you know, considering it *involves me*."

"Baby, I need you to calm down."

"Do not tell me to calm down, Thane!" she snapped.

"Shite," he hissed and dragged his hands down his face.

"Just how bad *is* this?"

In answer to her question, he grabbed the remote and turned on the television. He didn't have to scroll far to find the first of several channels where Thane and his love life were the top stories of the day.

"Who is this mysterious woman you ask?" a young female anchor queried.

Sydney lowered herself slowly onto the sofa and watched as a group of men and women who didn't know her discussed rumor and innuendo relating to who she was to Thane, complete with grainy and often times blurry photographs. "That was at the restaurant," she whispered.

"Aye, love. And at the premiere, and as we're leaving the train station. Wallace intercepted a couple of drones as they tried to fly over the house."

"Intercepted, how?"

"He shot them down. He's always been an avid pheasant hunter."

Sydney covered her face with a groan. "I'm sorry, honey."

"Why the hell are you sorry? My people should have stopped this."

"*Or*, I should have stayed home instead of going to the premiere. I didn't have to have a total meltdown on a public sidewalk outside of the restaurant, either." She shook her head. "I just wasn't thinking. Not to mention, if I'd traveled separately, you could have probably avoided all of this."

"Bloody hell, Sydney, this is not your fault."

"If it's not my fault, why are you snapping at me?"

He took a deep breath and sat beside her, linking his fingers with hers. "I'm sorry, love. I don't mean to snap. With the worries your uncle has and the fact that the media are jackals, I'm concerned for your safety and when I'm concerned for your safety, I tend to get a little irritated."

"A little?" she challenged, but gave him a slight smile.

"Perhaps a little more than a little."

"Why are you so concerned?"

"Because your uncle believes you or Lucy might have a stalker."

"What?" She gasped. "Seriously?"

Thane nodded, pulling her against his chest. "It's part of the reason he was happy to have you come with me this weekend. It means he can watch Lucy a little closer and I can watch you."

"Why didn't he tell me?"

"Because he wanted to be sure first. He hasn't gotten to where he is by jumping to conclusions." He rubbed her back. "We're going to sort this out, sweetheart. I promise."

She lifted her head to look at him. "Do you think it was a reporter standing by the cottage?"

"I don't know. Wallace has sent the cigarette butts off for DNA analysis. If we can find the man, we will."

She relaxed against him again. "So, you worrying about the media thing isn't about me dating you?"

"No," he assured. "It's because they are mapping our movements to a certain degree. I need to keep you somewhat sheltered until we figure this out, but if reporters are following us, snapping photos and such, I can't do that. I'm going to stay in my London flat until we sort this out, though."

"You have a London flat?"

"Aye, lass. In Kensington."

"Then why were you at the hotel?" she asked.

"My flat's small and the hotel was the only place to accommodate everyone. I wanted to be close."

"Oh," she said. "Makes sense."

"If you want to stay with me, you're welcome to. Just let me know."

"No, I'll stay with my aunt and uncle."

She felt him stiffen and bit back a grin, grateful he couldn't see her expression.

"If that's what you want, love."

Sydney couldn't stay stoic for long and burst into quiet giggles.

"You bloody wee ratbag," he accused and pushed her onto her back, grabbing her waist and squeezing.

"Thane!" she yelled as she roared with laughter. "Stop, I'm going to pee."

He continued to tickle her until she found a way to reciprocate. He was too quick for her, though, and pinned both her hands above her head, running his free hand down her cheek. "You've got an evil streak, I see."

She licked her lips and nodded. "Remember that."

Thane grinned and leaned close, running his nose gently against hers. "I have a sure fire way to counteract your evil streak, sweetheart."

"You do?"

"Aye, lass." He covered her lips with his and released her arms so she could wrap them around his neck.

Sydney opened her mouth to deepen the kiss and slid her fingers into his hair. *You're driving me nuts, mister movie star.*

He broke the kiss with a grimace and dropped his forehead to hers. "One month, love."

"I know." She kissed him quickly and pushed him up. "I stick with my opinion about all of this sucking, though."

He smiled and nodded. "Agreed."

"I know we need to go back early, but can early mean Monday? I'd love one more day in our bubble before we have to get back to reality."

"Of course," he whispered. "Perhaps we can take a walk on the Leith Dock tomorrow. It's beautiful at night all lit up and we can eat dinner at one of Brodie's restaurants."

"Brodie?"

"Brodie Gunnach. He's one of the princes. He owns several clubs and restaurants around Scotland, and one of them is on the water. It'll be private and we won't be bothered. Plus the food's outstanding."

She bit back a yawn. "I would *love* that."

"Sleep, baby," he whispered, and she did.

* * *

Sydney was excited to be going to dinner, even with the possibility of the paparazzi finding them. The rain had stopped and the night was clear enough to see the stars, which meant they could explore a little.

Thane knocked, pushing the door further open. "Are you ready, love?"

She glanced at him over her shoulder as she secured an earring. "Almost."

Crossing his arms, he leaned against the doorjamb. "You look beautiful, sweetheart."

She'd pulled her hair into a long braid to the side and wore jeans, knee-high boots, and a flowy dark red blouse.

"Thank you." Sydney turned to face him, assessing him in all his glory. "You look pretty delectable yourself."

He wore dark jeans, motorcycle boots, and a black, long-sleeved thermal henley. With his black leather jacket, he looked more *Sons of Anarchy* than immortal Viking.

"I found out Brodie and his mate Payton will actually be there tonight and have invited us to sit with them, but only if you don't mind. If you want to be alone, that's fine as well."

She smiled and grabbed her jacket and purse. "Sounds fun."

"Are you sure?"

"Yes, honey." She leaned in and kissed him quickly. "I'm sure."

"Damn."

Sydney cocked her head. "If you don't want to, we don't have to."

"I'm torn."

"You are?"

"Aye. I want to see them, but I'd rather spend time alone with you."

"Then tell them 'no.'"

He gave her a cheeky grin. "And not have you to blame it on? No, that won't work."

"Oh, I see how it is." Sydney giggled. "Sorry, babe. I've never met a real life prince. Royalty trumps you tonight."

He grinned, grasping her hand. "Fair enough. But I want the promise of a make-out session on the sofa later."

"Well, duh," she retorted.

Thane laughed and led her downstairs and out to the waiting car.

* * *

As Thane had promised, there wasn't an inkling of paparazzi anywhere near the restaurant. "How did Brodie manage this much privacy?" Sydney asked.

"He has a few on his staff who have the power of suggestion, so they are dismissed almost as quickly as they arrive. We know who's Cauld Ane and who's human, so it's easy to head them off at the pass."

"That's amazing."

Thane grinned as he opened the door and followed Sydney inside.

"Mr. Allen, welcome." A young woman with silky black hair and pale skin smiled at them. She reminded Sydney of Lucy Liu, freckles and all. She was gorgeous. "Mr. Gunnach is expecting you."

"Thank you, Paige," Thane said, and laid his hand on Sydney's lower back, guiding her in front of him.

You've been here before.

Aye, lass. Several times.

She glanced around the room. *Is there anyone who works here who isn't gorgeous?*

I wouldn't know, sweetheart.

She glanced at him over her shoulder. "Smart man."

"Thane!"

Sydney followed the sound of the booming voice and stepped back a little. A tall blond man rushed for Thane and picked him up in a bear hug. "You bloody bastard, how the hell are you?"

Thane laughed and shook his head. "I'll be great when you put me down, ye daft bampot." The man lowered Thane and he reached for Sydney's hand. "Sydney, this is Brodie and his mate, Payton."

Sydney hadn't seen the gorgeous redhead, considering she was behind Brodie and he was huge. Like WWE huge. He was handsome...almost model pretty, but she also could imagine him on an ancient battlefield, a sword in one hand and a dagger in the other, able to kill a man with his bare hands.

"Ignore him, Sydney." Payton smiled and gave Brodie's bottom a gentle smack. "I try to when he's being rude."

"Was I being rude, love?" Brodie asked with a cheeky lilt to his voice.

Sydney shook Payton's hand and chuckled. "It's lovely to meet you both."

"Come and sit by me. It's date night, our little boy is home with Kade and Samantha, and I'm dying for some adult conversation."

"Hey, I'm adult conversation," Brodie countered.

Payton grinned. "You keep telling yourself that, love."

Sydney giggled and took the seat next to Payton. Thane sat next to her and Brodie sat on the other side of Payton.

"Connall and Pepper may be here later," Payton said. "They're visiting Megan before the baby comes, so they said they'll stop by if they have time."

Connall is Brodie's brother. Megan is Pepper's mother. They're almost ready to have their second child.

Sydney squeezed Thane's leg in thanks.

Paige arrived at the table and smiled at Thane and Sydney. "May I get you both something to drink?"

"I'd love a merlot, please," Sydney said.

"Whatever costs Brodie the most money," Thane said.

Paige chuckled. "Perfect."

She left and, before the group could fall into comfortable conversation, another tall blond man walked in, a gorgeous blonde woman, her small frame overtaken by her large round belly, at his side. Payton let out an excited squeak and shot out of her seat, pulling Sydney with her before hugging the woman gently. "Pepper! You made it."

"We did. Cody was *not* happy that mommy and daddy were leaving, but we prevailed." Pepper glanced over at her husband. "Remember when he couldn't speak? I liked those days."

Connall grinned. "Aye, love. I do."

"Pepper, this is Sydney," Payton offered.

"You're the one on the video singing with Fallen Crown," Sydney blurted out.

"Guilty," Pepper said.

"Sorry. Sometimes I forget to filter."

Pepper chuckled. "I know a little about that."

"Well, you were amazing."

"Thank you. I understand you're from my neck of the woods."

"You're from California?" Sydney asked.

"By way of Georgia, yes. I lived in San Jose until second grade."

Sydney smiled. "Willow Glen until about ten years ago."

"Holy cow, me too. We lived on Louise Avenue."

"Minnesota... well, until we moved to Menlo Park."

"We were practically neighbors."

Sydney nodded. "Definitely."

"And now you're here." Pepper smiled. "If you have any questions about your bonding night or anything, let me know. I was human as well."

Sydney gasped. "You were?"

Pepper nodded.

"I have a million questions," she admitted. "But I didn't realize Thane had told everyone about me."

"He didn't," Pepper said. "We feel your connection."

"I don't understand."

"I don't know if I can explain it, honestly, but there's a vibration of sorts with the two of you, and Con and I knew you were mates."

"Wow, this is all really bizarre."

I'll help you sort it out, love. Don't panic on me now.

She glanced over at Thane and gave him a reassuring smile. *I'm not panicking, just a little overwhelmed.*

She saw him relax, so she turned back to Pepper.

"The telepathy part freaked me out at first," Pepper admitted.

"Yeah, it's super weird," Sydney admitted. "I'm still not sure how it works."

"It's something to do with empathy. It's actually a gift humans and Cauld Ane share, so it's why you can speak telepathically." She smiled. "You'll have some very passionate arguments as well."

Sydney groaned. "Great, something to look forward to."

"I'll make sure we exchange numbers so you can call me if you want to."

Sydney smiled. "Thanks, I appreciate it."

"Sitting down now, love," Connall ordered, and Pepper rolled her eyes.

"I'm coming, I'm coming," Pepper droned. "Sydney, this is Connall. I thought he'd be a little less of a fusser with the second kid." She lowered her voice. "He's worse."

Sydney giggled and Connall shook her hand. "It's nice to meet you, Sydney."

"Nice to meet you too."

"Come on, love," he said, and guided Pepper to the table.

Sydney felt Thane's arm slide around her waist from behind as he kissed her temple. "You okay?"

She turned to face him with a grin. "I'm fine. Don't worry, honey. I'm not going anywhere."

He stroked her cheek. "If you find this at all overwhelming, you let me know. We can leave. I have a bottle of wine waiting and a movie queued up."

"Nice try." Sydney rolled her eyes. "I don't want to leave. I want to get to know your friends."

"Damn it," he breathed out, kissing her quickly before leading her back to her seat.

"When are you due, Pepper?" Sydney asked.

"A couple of weeks. Our three-year-old is with Grandma and Grandpa right now, so we have a rare night off."

"How long are you staying?" Thane asked.

"We're staying through the birth. Provided this little one comes before Liam's big birthday." She laid her hands on her belly.

"Kade and Sam have been here for the last month and have to stay for another few weeks, and since she's bossy and my best friend as well as my sister-in-law, I am required to stay put until Doctor Sam delivers the next baby Gunnach into the world."

Payton giggled. "She's not a very good patient herself though, and she's also going to have another baby in few weeks, so she's a little more hormonal than normal."

"Sweetheart, can we please refrain from discussing the queen's hormones?" Brodie interjected.

"Lighten up, Brodie," Pepper teased. "You know if Sam heard you refer to her as the queen, she'd have a coronary... or throw something at your head." She focused back on Sydney. "Sam has been a pain in my butt for the last three months, so discussion about her hormones is open season. Back me up, Pay."

"Well, I wouldn't say pain in the butt," Payton countered.

"That's because you're nice... and she's nicer to you than to me."

Payton laughed. "She's nice to you."

Pepper grinned. "Sure, let's go with that."

"I take it you've known Samantha for a while," Sydney said.

Pepper nodded. "Since second grade. She's the best friend I've ever had."

"Aw, that's sweet."

"Until she's a pain in the butt."

Payton choked on her wine and let out a surprised laugh. "Bloody hell, Pepper, you have to warn me when you're going to make me laugh."

"Comic relief and eye candy, Pay. I just do my thing, hon, I don't plan it."

Payton shook her head as she took several deep breaths. Brodie slipped his hand to the back of her neck and she leaned against him.

"Sam was also human, by the way," Pepper added.

"Should we just start introducing you and Sam as the ex-humans?" Payton asked.

"Sounds too harsh. You know, like when we started saying pre-owned car, rather than used car? How about pre-mated?"

Payton wrinkled her nose. "Too close to cremated."

Pepper laughed. "You might have a point."

Sydney forced a smile as she watched the two women. She really missed her mom. Thane took her hand, giving it a gentle squeeze. *I've got you, love.*

Thank you.

The rest of the dinner passed all too quickly for Sydney. For the first time in a very long time, she felt part of something. She'd never been one to have a lot of friends in high school and college, probably because she became more withdrawn after her father died. But tonight, seeing how much this family adored Thane, and how they treated him like one of their own and, by extension, her as well, she felt like she could be totally herself. Now she just had to figure out who she was in this new world she was falling in love with.

"Do you want to walk the dock, love?" Thane asked as they filed out of the restaurant.

"I'd love to," she said.

"We'll say goodnight here," Payton said, and hugged Sydney. "But please say we'll do this again."

"Definitely," she promised.

Pepper hugged her as well. "As soon as our next moose kid comes into the world, we'll be having a little party, so I hope you'll be there."

"I'm sure we'll make it happen."

They finished off their good nights, and Thane wrapped an arm around Sydney as the other couples left them. "They are so awesome, honey."

Thane nodded and guided her along the sparkling waterfront. "Aye, love, they are. They're certainly more family than friends."

They didn't speak for the longest time. Just listened to the sound of the water lapping against the dock as they walked along the sidewalk. Sydney couldn't help a smile as she pulled Thane to a stop and looped her arms around his neck. "Thank you."

"For?"

"For everything." She stroked his hair and smiled up at him. "I know I can't rely on anyone else to make me happy, but you do."

Thane squeezed her waist. "You were worth the wait."

"I was?"

"Aye, lass." He chuckled. "We are prepared to wait. It's something ingrained in us from birth, because we only have one mate, but some of us wait longer than others, and I always wondered who you'd be. I couldn't have hoped for better, sweetheart. I love everything about you and I can't wait to discover more. God blessed me beyond measure with you, Sydney."

"Thane," she whispered, blinking back tears.

"I have something for you," he said, and reached into his jacket pocket, pulling out a black leather box and kneeling before her. "Sydney Roslyn Warren, will you do me the honor of marrying me?"

She gasped, covering her mouth with her hands and nodding. He stood and slipped the ring on her finger and she threw herself against him, kissing him with abandon. "I love you so much."

He held her for several minutes until Sydney decided she needed to see the ring. Another gasp escaped her lips as the giant diamond glittered under the dock lights. "Wow."

"Do you like it?" he asked. "We can return it if it's not quite what you want."

"I love it."

The center diamond was emerald cut and the band was designed with intricate Celtic knots that wrapped around her finger. "It looks beautiful on you. I was worried seven carats would be too big for your hand, but it's perfect."

"Seven?" She shook her head. "Thane, that's too much."

"You don't like it?"

"I love it."

"Then it's perfect."

She sighed. "Well, as Mom always used to say, 'when it comes to houses and diamonds, it's never too big.'"

Thane chuckled. "Wise words."

She gripped his chin and stood on her tiptoes. "I love you."

"I love you, too." He leaned down and kissed her gently before walking her to the waiting car.

Sydney kept a firm hold on his hand as Wallace drove them home and once again fell asleep in Thane's arms, not waking once during the night.

CHAPTER TEN

MONDAY AFTERNOON, AFTER Sydney was forced to wait with Lucy while Thane and Uncle Cary talked alone, she was finally officially released into Thane's care. However, before that lovely bit of permission was given, her cousin Anson settled himself beside her on the sofa, plastering his best big brother face on, and taking her hand. He dropped his thumb onto her engagement ring and frowned.

"Antsy," Sydney said, using his nickname and trying not to whine. She knew what was coming.

"How much do you really know about this guy, Sid?"

"Enough."

"You met him a week ago and he's already proposed? Something's off, love."

"I appreciate your concern, Anson, I really do, but your dad had him totally checked out and, I may not have known him for long, but I *know* him. Trust me on that."

"But you're vulnerable right now and I don't think you're thinking clearly," he continued.

Sydney groaned and pulled her hand from his. "I love you, Antsy. I love you so much it hurts, and even sometimes so much I'd like to hurt you, but I promise you, I'm not as vulnerable as you think, and my eyes are wide open."

Anson laughed. "Alright, cousin, I tried."

"And I applaud your efforts."

He leaned in and hugged her before rising to his feet and heading back from whence he came. Sydney narrowed her eyes at Lucy. "Did you put him up to that?"

She let out a loud huff. "Why are you so quick to blame me for everything? Oh my god, Sid. I set you up with Thane, I sicced Anson on you. When will it ever end?"

"You did! You totally sicced him on me."

She rolled her eyes. "I didn't sic him, sic him on you. I just wanted to see your reaction when *he* asked you those questions."

Sydney sobered. "Are you worried?"

"Not anymore." Lucy shrugged.

Sydney sighed as she stood and moved to sit beside her cousin. "I'm okay, Luce. I promise. I love Thane and we're totally good."

Lucy grabbed Sydney's hand. "I just want you to be happy."

"I want the same for you, you know."

"I know." Lucy smiled. "I think I may have found him."

"I can't wait to meet him. We'll make that happen this week, okay?"

"You better."

"Sid?" Thane's voice took her focus.

Sydney turned toward the door and smiled up at him. "Everything sorted?"

"Aye, lass. We can go whenever you'd like," he said. "Lucy, are we meeting Zach this week?"

Lucy's face lit up. "Yes! When?"

"Thursday or Friday works for me, so if that's okay for everyone else, let's make a plan."

She clapped her hands. "I'll talk to Zach and work it out with Sid."

"Perfect." Thane smiled and focused back on Sydney. "Do you want to pack anything else?"

"Nope, I think I'm good. I can always come back if I realize I'm missing anything."

He held his hand out. "Shall we?"

Sydney hugged Lucy and then followed Thane out of the house. Once inside the SUV, she buckled up and stared at him.

"What?" he asked.

"Seriously?" she complained. "What did my uncle say?"

"I'd rather have this conversation over an expensive bottle of wine."

"That bad?"

He grimaced as he lifted her fingers to his lips. "Yeah, love, that bad."

"Well, shit," she whispered.

It didn't take long to arrive at Thane's flat. Sydney found her heart racing as Thane led her into the elevator and the doors closed behind them. His home was on the top two floors and close to three-thousand square feet.

"You said your apartment was small, honey. This is *not* small."

The building was historic, built sometime in the late 1700s, but his apartment had been renovated less than five years ago. There were three bedrooms, an office, a movie room, four and a half bathrooms, a huge kitchen and great room, and the view was a stunning near-three-sixty-degree view of the city.

He chuckled. "Still not quite big enough to accommodate everyone attached to the movie, however."

"Perhaps not."

"Make yourself at home, love. I'll pour some wine," Thane offered, and Sydney made her way to the windows overlooking High Street.

"How long have you lived here?" she called.

"I haven't really ever lived here, to be honest." He returned with a glass of merlot and handed it to her.

"Thanks," she said, and took a sip.

"I bought the top flat ten years ago, and then bought this one and combined them about five years ago. It's more of an investment than anything."

"Well, it's lovely." She tipped her glass toward him. "You have impeccable taste in pretty much everything."

Thane chuckled. "Thank you."

He took her hand and led her to the sofa and she carefully navigated herself onto it in order not to spill her wine. "How bad?"

Thane sighed and shook his head. "Your mother's accident... ah, wasn't an accident."

"Meaning?"

"It looks as though it may have been intentional."

"What?" she squeaked. Thane took her wine glass and set both of theirs on the table. Sydney was glad he did since her hands were shaking uncontrollably. "I thought the guy who hit her was drunk."

Thane shook his head. "No alcohol or drugs were found in his system, so the police think it could be murder. Your mother did make a report about the phone calls, so with all of the evidence piling up, it's pointing to homicide."

"I don't understand."

"Come here." He pulled her onto his lap and wrapped his arms around her.

She looped her arms around his neck and let his comfort seep into her. "Do they know for a fact it was murder?"

"It's looking that way, love. They followed the money. The man who hit her is a sixty-year-old, stage-four lung cancer patient who'd been given about six months to live. They'd exhausted all treatment options, and the police believe he did it for the money. He's still in a coma, but when they investigated him, they discovered a wire deposit of fifty-thousand dollars the day before the crash. The day *of* the crash, that fifty grand was transferred to an offshore account. When they searched his home, they found e-mails mapping out a plan to kill both of you. The police haven't been able to find *who* he was e-mailing just yet, but they're working on it. They believe his plan was to kill himself in the process, but he failed."

Sydney shuddered. "I was supposed to be with her."

"I know, love."

"Who was he?"

"Marvin Webster. Do you know him?"

She shook her head. "I've never heard of him."

"They're still working the case, which is why you're under lock and key for a little while."

"But we're all the way in England, Thane. Do the police really think whoever's behind this can find me here?"

He shrugged. "Neither your uncle nor I are willing to find out."

"When you say 'under lock and key,' do you mean literally or figuratively?"

"It means you don't go anywhere without me or one of my men. For the most part, love, it doesn't really change anything, I just need you to be aware of your surroundings and be on alert."

She sighed. "I can do that."

He grinned and kissed her gently. "Thank you."

She pushed away from him and rose to her feet.

"What, love?"

"I need to know what this feels like without you calming me," she admitted, and sat in the chair opposite him. The pain came hard and fast, stealing her breath. She burst into tears. Thane stood and rushed to her, but she raised a hand and shook her head.

"Sweetheart, I can help."

"I don't want you to help," she snapped. "Just give me some time, Thane, please. I have to feel this. All of it."

He frowned as he sat on the coffee table facing her, settling his elbows on his knees and watching her closely.

She closed her eyes and shut him out, letting the sobs wrack her as she tried to process the information she'd been given, but all she could think about was the beautiful and vibrant woman who'd been ripped away from her. Her mother had been her best friend.

The memory of her mother in her coffin flashed in her mind, the horrific injuries she'd suffered covered by makeup—she didn't look like her mom anymore. Sydney could almost pretend they'd made a mistake, but it wasn't a mistake. Her mother had been murdered. Someone had purposely taken her life, and they had wanted to take Sydney's as well. It was too much.

Strong arms wrapped around her and lifted her from the chair. "That's enough," Thane rasped.

She nodded into his neck and let him carry her to the bedroom, her emotions calming as he laid her on the mattress and stretched out beside her. He didn't break contact as he pulled her onto his chest and kissed her hair. Sydney ran her finger over his heart and took a deep breath. "Who would hate us enough to want us dead?"

"I don't know, love, but we're going to find out."

"If I hadn't had a headache... if I'd gone with her... maybe we would have stopped somewhere for dinner. Or what if at the last minute, we decided to go to the movies?"

"Shh, don't, Sydney. You'll drive yourself mad with the what-ifs."

"They took the best person I've ever known from this earth, Thane."

He gave her a gentle squeeze. "I know, baby."

"They have to suffer."

"We'll find them, sweetheart. I promise."

She leaned up to meet his eyes. "I want them to suffer."

"I heard you, baby."

"And you'll make that happen?"

"No, sweetheart, I won't. But they *will* be brought to justice."

"That's not good enough, Thane." She pushed off the bed. "They need to hurt like they made her hurt. Like they're making me hurt now!"

He sat on the edge of the bed and watched her.

"Why are you just sitting there?" she bellowed. "Say something!"

Thane reached for her hand, pulling her between his legs and wrapping his arms around her.

"Let me go," she snapped. She tried to push away again, but he held firm.

"No, love, just settle," he demanded, and slid one hand behind her neck, squeezing gently. "We're going to find whoever did this to yer mum. I promise. And we're going to make sure whoever did it is brought to justice, but we're no' going to torture anyone. I know you're in pain right now, and you're entitled to feel however you feel, so you rage all you want. I'm here."

She fell against him and squeezed her eyes shut. "I hate them."

"I know, baby."

"What if they can't find—"

He frowned. "Don't go there, love."

"But—"

"No, Sydney. We *will* find them. I promise."

Sydney sighed. "I feel like I'm just finding out she's dead all over again."

"I know, love."

She bit her lip. "You make me feel calm."

"I know, love," he repeated.

"That's not a good thing," she accused.

"I know that as well." He smiled and stroked her cheek. He held her for several minutes until she finally relaxed against him. "What do you want to do?"

"Honestly?" She wrinkled her nose. "Right now, I want to eat my feelings."

Thane chuckled. "What do you need?"

"Chocolate and wine."

"Lucky for you, I have both." He patted her bottom. "I'm going to stay close to you tonight, love. I know you want to feel everything, but I can't watch you go down that road again. Do you understand?"

She nodded. "I don't really want to either."

"Good. Come on, let's have some chocolate therapy."

Sydney followed him back out to the kitchen where he found some form of delectable chocolate pastry his housekeeper or whoever had left for him in the fridge.

Just before midnight, he helped her fall asleep and Sydney prayed it would last the night.

CHAPTER ELEVEN

TWO WEEKS LATER, Sydney's irritation at being relegated to Thane's or her aunt and uncle's homes was beginning to wear on her. There were still no updates from the police and she wanted out, so Thane reluctantly agreed to dinner with Lucy and Zach. Of course, it had to be at a restaurant he approved of, meaning, it had to be one he had the star power to shut down for an evening.

Sydney didn't much care what he had to do to give them a night out with her cousin, so she didn't voice her opinion on the amount of money he was spending by shutting down a popular restaurant for an evening... well, she didn't voice it *much*.

"Sid, are you ready?" Thane called from the hallway.

She stepped out of the bedroom and smiled. "I'm coming. Keep your pants on."

"Two more weeks, love, and I'll be ripping them off."

Sydney giggled and kissed him quickly. "Promises, promises."

Thane ushered her out of the apartment and down to the garage where Wallace waited with the car. Arriving at the back entrance of the restaurant, they were secreted in and showed to their table where Lucy and Zach already sat.

Lucy jumped up and made a run for Sydney. "You're actually here!" she exclaimed as she hugged her. "I didn't know if it would happen."

Sydney chuckled. "Sorry it's been so nuts."

"I get it." Lucy smiled and hugged Thane.

"I'm Zach."

"Oh, sorry," Lucy said with a laugh and faced him. "Yes, this is Zach."

Zach was tall with dark hair and deep brown, almond-shaped eyes. To say he was gorgeous was an understatement. His Asian features and height gave him model good looks and the fact he obviously worked out, made him all that more attractive.

Careful, love.

Sydney smiled up at Thane. *You're still hotter, but stay out of my head, mister movie star.*

Thane shook Zach's hand and Sydney followed suit.

"Come and sit," Zach said. "Apparently, we have the place to ourselves. Must be nice to be the biggest movie star on the planet."

Thane chuckled, but for a second, it was a little awkward.

"Zach, love. Filter," Lucy ordered.

Zach laughed. "Right, sorry. I tend to say what I'm thinking."

Sydney sat across from Lucy while Thane sat across from Zach and, once the server took their drink orders, they studied the menu.

"So, Lucy tells me you're from Cali," Zach said. "Which part?"

"San Jose."

"No shit?" he said. "Me too. East side."

"Oh, wow, close. We lived in Willow Glen."

He chuckled. "You were on the good side of the tracks."

Sydney smiled. "Is there a bad side in this day and age? Everything costs a fortune."

"That's true. Did you go to Willow Glen?"

"No, Valley Christian."

"Oh-hoh, private school. Nice." He chuckled. "For me, it was Silver Creek."

"That's a good school," Sydney said.

"Yeah, it was okay."

"What made you come here?" Thane asked, laying his menu on his plate.

"I needed a change. Thought I could do a college exchange for a semester, but now that I've met this gorgeous woman"—he smiled at Lucy—"I'm thinking of making it a yearlong exchange."

Lucy blushed. "Which would be wonderful."

"It totally would, babe," he said, and kissed her.

Sydney focused on her menu again, a little surprised by the public display of affection...well, no, perhaps it was more that it was shudder-worthy PDA. The kiss showed so much tongue, Sydney wasn't sure if Zach was kissing her cousin or trying to find out how many licks it took to get to her chewy center.

Ugh, gross.

"Zach," Lucy admonished. "We're being rude."

"Right, sorry. You totally just carry me away, babe."

Oh, boy.

Thane squeezed her hand. *Romance is lost on you?*

That's not romance. That's just creepy.

He grinned, lifting her hand to his lips.

Oh, good, honey, perpetuate the creepy.

"So, Thane," Zach began again. "How'd you get into acting?"

"I kind of fell into it, to be honest, and it took off."

"Yeah, dude, that's an understatement."

Thane smiled. "I've been very lucky."

"Did you know Zach was a competitive surfer?" Lucy said.

Sydney smiled at her cousin's attempt to take the focus off Thane.

That explains the "dude" talk. I feel like I'm trapped inside Bill and Ted's Excellent Adventure.

"Where's your favorite place to surf?" Thane asked, squeezing Sydney's thigh.

"Whoa, man, that's hard to answer." He gave a stoner chuckle.

Stoner chuckle?

Sydney glanced at him. *Well it is!*

"There's this totally gnarly beach in New Zealand," Zach continued. "It's called Piha and the waves are righteous. Not as big as some places I've been, but totally worth it."

Lucy grinned. "Zach managed to travel all over the place for next to no money."

"That's impressive," Sydney said, a headache forming rapidly.

"Yeah, I got some sponsorships, stayed at youth hostels... that kind of stuff. It was awesome." He sipped his beer. "Even if I had the money to do it differently, I don't think I would have. What about you, Sydney? Growing up with such a rich dad must have meant travel, right?"

Really? Rich dad? Who is this guy?

Lucy gasped. "Zach!"

"What? It's just a question. Her dad's like the sixth richest man in America... it's not like it's a secret."

Thane threaded his fingers with hers, easing the pain in her skull. *Patience, love. Your cousin loves him.*

Sydney tried to stamp down her irritation "Dad traveled a lot for work, so we didn't have much family vacation time. Mom and I were kind of our own team."

"Hmm," he murmured. "You think he was "traveling," or steppin' out?"

"Zach!" Lucy snapped again.

Sydney scowled at Zach.

"I'm just kiddin'," Zach said.

Sweetheart, you okay?

Yep. Dandy. She forced a smile before facing Lucy. Lucy was studying her closely, but Sydney was glad her cousin didn't ask any questions.

Sydney suffered through dinner, rethinking her need to be out of the house. She wished she could click her heels together and be anywhere else, but Thane was right, Lucy adored this idiot, so she needed to at least try.

Idiot? Thane choked on a sip of wine and gave her a sideways glance. *Warn me next time you're feeling feisty.*

Or how about you just stay out of my head?

"Are you all right, Thane?" Lucy asked.

"Yes, lass, fine. Thank you."

He raised an eyebrow and kissed Sydney's cheek gently. *Behave.*

Suck it. She gave him a saccharin sweet smile and sipped her wine.

Dessert arrived and Sydney plowed into her cheesecake in an effort to get the night over with. If she had to endure Zach's inane Spicoli speak for much longer, she was sure she might snap. It was Lucy who called the dinner to an end.

"Is anyone up for a walk?" Lucy asked.

"I'm actually really tired," Sydney lied. "Raincheck?"

"Of course." Lucy hugged Sydney and whispered, "You hate him."

"I don't *hate* him."

"Yes you do." She pulled back with a frown. "Shit."

Sydney noticed Thane guide Zach away from them and focused back on Lucy. "I'm sorry."

"Don't be," she said with a sigh. "Now I have to dump him."

"No! Don't do that on my account."

"Lovey, you were the one and only test. I knew if you had an issue with him, he was gone. Remember when you visited freshman year of high school and totally hated George?"

Sydney nodded.

"Well, George got arrested for three rapes. Then, there was the Ellie thing, oh, and the Mr. Murray incident of two-thousand-and-seven."

"What's that supposed to mean?"

"Sid, you have this uncanny ability to get to the soul of a person. If they're rotten your body literally reacts to them. You're a human litmus test."

"How am I a human litmus test?" she asked.

"Because you get all emotional and headachy when you meet horrible people."

Sydney rolled her eyes. "Don't be dramatic."

"Sid, you met Ellie and immediately asked for ibuprofen, just like with George. You also refused to touch her. Same with

George. Ellie had just stolen diamonds from a jewelry store, and then, you remember Mr. Murray right."

Sydney shuddered. "The creepy teacher?"

"Yes. He was sleeping with multiple students in exchange for good grades. You know who's good and who's bad just by meeting them."

"I'm sure Zach's fine, Luce. He's just kind of a dooooood."

Lucy giggled. "Nah, he's gone. He wasn't very good in bed anyway."

"Lucy!" Sydney admonished. "Way TMI, babe."

She rolled her eyes. "I just wish you could have met him sooner. Now he's going to be a pain in the arse about me cutting him loose."

"Luce, really. Don't make your decision based on me."

"Okay, love." Lucy hugged her again.

"I'm serious," Sydney pressed.

"I promise."

Sydney narrowed her eyes, but knew she couldn't control what Lucy did, so gave her a quick nod and walked with her back to join the men. Thane wrapped an arm around her waist and pulled her close.

"It was great to meet you, Zach," Thane said, and shook his hand.

"You too, man. If you ever need a hot Asian guy for a movie, hook me up."

Thane chuckled. "I'll keep that in mind."

Like hell you will.

Thane patted Sydney's bottom before hugging Lucy. "Good to see you, Lucy."

"You too, Thane. I'm sure I'll see you sooner than later."

Thane smiled. "That's the plan."

Sydney tried not to stiffen as Zach pulled her in for a bear hug, falling against Thane in relief when Zach released her. She waited until she and Thane were in the car before groaning out loud. "That was gross."

Thane threw his head back and laughed. "You look like a toddler who just ate a lemon for the first time."

Sydney blushed. "Sorry. I know I'm being dramatic, but that guy gives me the willies."

"Willies, eh?"

She grimaced. "I'm sorry, honey. I didn't mean to be so ungracious to him."

"You have nothing to be sorry for. He was kind of a jerk." He squeezed her hand. "Shall we head back? Are you tired?"

"A bit, but..."

Thane chuckled again. "Making out before sleep?"

"Well, duh."

CHAPTER TWELVE

SYDNEY PULLED HER hair into a ponytail as she walked down the hallway and into the living room. She'd just changed into pajamas and washed the makeup off her face and now she wanted wine and make-out time with Thane. He was standing by one of the windows, his phone to his ear, and he appeared to be listening intently.

She made her way to him and he opened his free arm for her to slide against him, which she did. He gave her a gentle squeeze and she settled her chin on his chest so she could watch his expression.

"Aye, no. Aye. Pam, it's done, don't let them bully or manipulate you. They knew what they were doing and now they're going through you to try and change it. Aye. Full authority." He chuckled. "Aye, lass. Turn your phone off. Aye. We'll talk in a couple of weeks. If I need you, I'll send you an e-mail. Okay. Good. 'Bye."

"Everything okay?"

"Pam's getting some pushback from a few of the magazines and she's trying to be nice about it. I just gave her permission not to be." He stroked her hair. "Now, I have a question for you."

"Ask away."

"The little prince turns one just about a week after your birthday and Samantha wants to know if you'd like to go through the conversion at the castle. Pepper will be there, along with the staff who have all gone through the process with them, so they can keep you comfortable."

"Translation: if I go with you to their castle, it's an impenetrable force, and that means I will be safer there than anywhere and you'll feel better."

Thane chuckled. "Exactly."

Sydney smiled and looked up at him. "I'm fine with that as long as it's not inconvenient for anyone."

"She wouldn't have offered if it was."

"Then it's fine by me."

He grinned and leaned down to kiss her, pushing her onto her back. "Good answer."

"When do we go?"

"A couple of days before your birthday, however, my sister has threatened murder if I don't let you out this weekend."

Sydney giggled. "I desperately need some clothes, honey, so I would love time with your sister if you can make it work."

Thane kissed her neck. "When you're all sweetness and light like this, Sydney, I wonder what you're up to."

"Me? Why would I be up to anything?"

He narrowed his eyes. "Why indeed?"

Sydney sighed. "I'm trying to ask nicely to go shopping with your sister, rather than demand you get off my back since I'm a grown-ass adult and should be allowed to do whatever the hell I want to."

Thane dropped his head onto her shoulder and laughed. "Shite, love, you're hilarious."

She couldn't help but smile. "So, what time shall I expect your sister on Friday?"

"I'll ring her tonight."

She slid her hands into his hair. "Thank you."

Thane raised his head and kissed her. "Well played, sweetheart."

Sydney giggled.

* * *

Connall came awake as Pepper grabbed for him. He felt pain slice through her as she experienced a contraction. He sat up before he was completely awake. "Pepper?" he whispered.

"She's coming, baby."

Connall knifed off the bed and grabbed his phone. "She's early."

"I know it. Just like her brother." Pepper took a deep breath and let it out. "Little cretin."

He put the phone to his ear as he watched Pepper closely. "Gillian, aye, she's in labor now. How far apart are the contractions, love?"

"About four minutes," she said, and took another deep breath.

"Four minutes. Right, see you soon. She'll be here in ten minutes," he said as he pulled on a pair of sweats.

"Crap."

"What, baby?"

"I think my water just broke. I'm soaked."

"All right, love." He moved to Pepper's side of the bed and helped her up. "Let's get you out of these wet things."

He helped her into clean clothes and guided her to the bench at the end of the bed just as another contraction hit and she cried out in pain. Connall knelt in front of her and took her hands. "You ready?"

She shook her head. "I need a little more time."

He chuckled as he worked to ease her pain. "She's obviously like her mother. Unpredictable and totally on her own schedule."

Pepper dropped her forehead to his. "Bite me."

"It's a compliment, love."

"Oh, well, then bite me in a good way." Connall laughed and Pepper gripped his shoulders. "We still don't have a name."

He sighed. "I know, love."

"She needs a name."

"Let's look at her and then decide," he suggested.

Before she could respond, Gillian, the royals' Cauld Ane OB/GYN, breezed into the room, followed by Samantha and Payton.

"Sam, you're supposed to be resting," Pepper admonished.

"I can't miss my niece's birth, Pep," Samantha said.

"Where's Kade?"

"In the hall with Brodie."

"I swear to Buddha, Sam, if you feel uncomfortable at all," Pepper started, but a contraction had her losing her breath.

"Okay, love," Connall soothed. "It's all right."

"Bed's all set," Payton said, and made her way to Pepper. "Ready to have our wee girl?"

Pepper squeezed her eyes shut. "Not at all."

"Settle her on the bed, Your Highness," Gillian instructed. "I'll examine her there."

"Aye." Connall lifted Pepper quickly and gently from the bench and laid her on the bed, keeping contact with her to ease the pain.

Payton and Samantha turned on lights and then Samantha took a seat with a scowl. "I heard you the first forty times you demanded it, Kade," she called.

Pepper cried out and Payton took her hand. Connall saw his mate's hair darken faster than it had with Cody.

"Pepper," Payton said quietly. "Calm yourself, love."

"*Hvers vegna? Er hárið aftur orðið rautt??*" (Why? Is my hair red again?)

Connall nodded and squeezed her hand. "*Já.*"

Pepper's hair lightened again, although, it was still darker than was safe. Pepper ripped her hand from Connall's. "*Ekki snerta mig!*" she snapped.

"Shite," Connall hissed.

"*Fyrirgefðu, elskan mín,*" Pepper whispered, and took his hand as her hair went back to blonde.

"There's nothing to forgive, love."

She burst into tears and grabbed Connall's shirt. "*Ég vil þetta barn út!*" (I want this baby out of me!)

"*Bráðum, elskan. Ég lofa.*" (Soon, sweetheart. I promise.)

"Here we go," Samantha warned.

Pepper gritted her teeth as another contraction hit her. She screamed and ripped Connall's shirt down the middle.

Payton gasped. "Again?"

When Pepper gave birth to Cody, she tore five of Connall's shirts. She'd had a difficult time controlling her pain and it had forced her super-strength abilities to the forefront. Luckily, her firestarter abilities hadn't surfaced. Connall hoped she'd be able to control herself a little more during this birth, but he wasn't holding out hope.

"I'm prepared this time, lass," Connall said, and smiled.

"I'm okay," Pepper said, this time in English.

Gillian smiled. "Ten centimeters, fully effaced."

"Are you ready to push, sweetheart?"

Pepper nodded, her hair now fully back to blonde. "Yep."

It took three pushes and twenty minutes to bring baby Chelsea into the world and Connall knew beyond a shadow of a doubt that he was in big trouble. The baby looked just like her mother, and since he couldn't say no to her, discipline was going to be a major issue for him in the future.

"Och, lassie," he crooned as Pepper held her. "You're going to cause me a lot of trouble."

Pepper giggled as she stroked the baby's cheek. "Yes, you will, Chelsea Samantha Gunnach."

Samantha gasped and sat on the edge of the bed. "You named her after me?"

"You're my sister and my best friend... duh."

Samantha laughed, leaning over to kiss the baby. "I love you."

"Love you too, honey."

"Everything looks great, Pepper," Gillian said. "You're already healing, so let's get Chelsea weighed and measured and then we'll see if she'll eat."

"I'll take her, love," Connall said, and cradled his little girl in his arms for a moment. "My beloved wee lassie, may God's blessings be heaped upon you, and I pray I'm the father you need to raise you to be just like your Mum." He kissed her head and handed her off to Gillian before turning to find Pepper, Samantha, and Payton crying. "What's the matter?"

"Nothing," Pepper said, wiping her eyes. "That was just so unbelievably sweet."

He chuckled and leaned down to kiss her gently. "You are a rock star, my love. Thank you."

"I didn't kill you this time," Pepper said, surprised. "And I only ripped one shirt."

"Aye, lass, you were amazing."

She giggled and kissed him again. Once the baby was settled at Pepper's breast, she ate a little and fell asleep quickly, so Brodie and Kade said hello to their new niece and then took their mates home.

Gillian stayed for about an hour to make sure all was okay before also leaving to head back to Brodie and Payton's. She was sticking around for Liam's party, and then also staying for the birth of the new prince.

Connall and Pepper decided not to wake Cody, but as soon as he was up and ready for the day, he met his new sister and the little family took some bonding time.

CHAPTER THIRTEEN

Elspie arrived just before noon on Friday. She pulled Sydney in for a tight sisterly hug and then greeted her brother. Wallace set her bags in the guestroom and promised to bring the car around when the ladies were ready to leave.

"I have orders from Mum and Ainsley."

"Orders?" Thane asked.

"Aye. There's a couple of things they want from that little boutique outside the mall. You know, A Touch in Time?"

"Since I'm a man, I can't say I do."

Eslpie giggled. "Well, if I find what they want, I'm going to lie and say I couldn't then give them to them for Christmas," she confided. "They're so bloody hard to buy for that it'll serve them right."

Thane chuckled. "Your secret's safe with me as long as my name's on the card."

Elspie jabbed a finger toward him with a laugh. "So predictable, brother."

"Are we eating before we go?" Thane asked.

"You're not coming," Elspie said emphatically.

"I vote we eat now," Sydney said. "I'm starving."

Elspie grinned. "I'm ready if you are."

Thane sighed. "What will I do while you're gone?"

Sydney and Elspie looked at each other. "Honey, you'll be fine," Sydney said. "You can survive a few hours without me."

"At least let me ride with you."

Elspie let out a snort. "Oh, how the mighty have fallen."

"What's that supposed to mean?"

"My very independent little brother suddenly can't go a few hours without his mate."

"I'm man enough to admit when I'm whipped," Thane retorted, pulling Sydney close. "Oh, baby, please let me come with you." He made lip smacking noises and buried his head in her neck.

Sydney giggled, trying to break away from his attack. "You're insane."

"Insanely in love with you," he said, releasing her.

"Charmer." Sydney leaned up on her tiptoes and kissed him. "Why don't you meet us for dinner?"

"Yeah?"

"Yeah." She giggled. "Make a reservation somewhere you approve of and we'll meet you there."

"Okay, love. I'll text you the particulars."

"Okay." She grabbed Elspie's hand. "Let's go before he changes his mind. We'll eat while we're out."

His sister laughed and they rushed out of the apartment.

* * *

Elspie led Sydney through store after store and Sydney honestly thought her legs might fall off by the time they were leaving the eighth. She'd never been a big fan of shopping—she did most of her purchases online—but Elspie had unlimited money and even worse, unlimited energy.

Damian, one of Thane's security men, followed them throughout the mall, and although he didn't say a word, Sydney was sure he must be bored out of his mind. Thane had also sent Niko who drove for them, but he was currently loading the car with their latest purchases.

"Did you hear that Connall and Pepper had their wee princess?" Elspie asked.

"We did." Sydney grinned. "Niall called Thane. She was early, huh?"

"Aye. By about a week. I have a feeling the queen will labor shortly as well."

"Really?"

"Aye. It happens with us women when we are pregnant at the same time. Now that there's a familial bond, we have our babies within weeks or even days of each other sometimes."

"What if they're not ready to come? Isn't that dangerous?"

Elspie smiled. "The bairns are fine. I imagine our bodies know what they're doing."

"I would hope so," Sydney murmured.

"We must get you something for your bonding night," Elspie decreed.

Sydney widened her eyes. "Like what?"

"Something sexy."

Sydney felt heat creep up her neck. "No offense, Elspie, but I'm not sure how Thane will feel if his sister picks me out something sexy for our bonding night."

Elspie giggled. "Don't tell him."

"I don't know how *I* feel about it."

"If you really don't want to, I will respect your wishes," she said, and took Sydney's hand. "We all just want you to feel comfortable, but with the loss of your parents, we also want you to know that you have family as well. We already adore you and Mum especially, wants you to know that."

Sydney blinked back tears. "That's really sweet, Elspie. Thank you."

Elspie smiled and guided Sydney toward the lingerie section.

Sydney, are you okay, love?

Yes. Your sister's just being very sweet.

He chuckled. *Well, that's a first.*

I won't tell her that. Sydney smiled. *She wants to help me pick out something sexy for our bonding night.*

I wholeheartedly approve.

You don't think it's weird?

If she were picking something sexy for me *to wear on our bonding night, then that would be weird.*

Sydney bit back a giggle. *You have a point. Okay, I'll find something mind blowing.*

Red.

Something mind blowing in red.

Thank you, love.

"What about this?" Elspie asked, and held up a barely there teddy in green.

Sydney shook her head. "He wants red."

She raised an eyebrow. "Telepathy has its good and bad points, right?"

Sydney smiled. "Mostly good I think...except when he refuses to stay out of my head."

"Marsh is the same way. Although, for us, it's not something strange. We're raised to expect and understand it."

"I suppose you are. That's kind of a mind bend." Sydney slid a few hangers back as she riffled through the choices. "Our kids will have that perspective as well. That's really cool."

"It is."

"What about this?" Sydney held up a red lacy nightie.

"Oh, that's lovely." Elspie smiled. "I'm going to see if I can find something as well while you try that on."

Sydney blushed. "Okay, be out in a bit."

Sydney ended up buying both the red and a similar one in blue, before they realized it was time to meet Thane at the restaurant.

On the way out of the shopping center, Sydney was distracted by the strangest little hole-in-the-wall shop that had random little tchotchkes covering shelves and tables all over the space. She was drawn to the "awards" shelf and couldn't stop a giggle when she found a gold plastic Oscar with "Best Lover" on the prize plate.

"Elspie, look." Sydney held up the statue.

"Oh, my word." Elspie giggled.

"Correct me if I'm wrong, but Thane's never won an Oscar, right?"

Elspie shook her head. "No, no he hasn't."

"Bonding night gift, check."

"No, that's what the nightie's for, love. Wait until the ceremony."

"You're a genius."

Elspie rubbed her fingernails on her shirt. "Tell me something I don't know."

Sydney grinned and paid for her little gem and then they headed out to the waiting car.

"Do you know where we're going?" Elspie asked Sydney as they headed away from the shopping center.

"Thane said a place called Kaylee, I think," Sydney said.

"Oh! Cèilidh." Elspie grinned. "It's one of Prince Brodie's properties. It's a new club downtown and it's virtually impossible to get into. We're lucky Brodie and Thane are such close friends."

Sydney nodded. "I'm just looking forward to seeing Thane. Is it strange that I miss him so much?"

"Not at all," Elspie assured. "Marsh is flying in tonight because I'm missing him. He's dropping the kids off at Mum and Da's and catching the first flight out."

Sydney chuckled. "So, even after years of being together, you still feel that way?"

"Aye."

"That's so lovely."

"Aye, love, 'tis."

The car pulled up to the back of the club and their doors were opened. Sydney let out a quiet squeak when Thane leaned in and pulled her out, wrapping his arms around her and lifting her off her feet.

"Hi, love. Bloody hell, I missed you," he said between kisses.

Sydney giggled, sliding her hands into his hair. "Pretty sure I missed you more."

"How do you figure?" He lowered her to the ground. "I've had to pine away the afternoon without you. You got to do something fun."

"You're right in theory," she countered. "But retail therapy didn't help distract me, so *obviously* I win this argument."

"Okay, love. I'll let you have that."

"Thank you."

"Are you hungry?" he asked.

"Starving."

"Brodie organized a private room for us, so we don't have to worry about cameras."

"That was nice of him."

"Aye." Thane grinned. "Els? As soon as you're done snoggin' yer mate, we'd like to eat."

"Marsh is here?" Sydney asked, unable to see behind the car.

Elspie tugged her mate out from behind the car, her face a little red, more than likely from Marsh's beard. "You're sneaky, brother."

Thane laughed. "I can't take any of the blame, love. Marsh took care of the details, I just picked him up."

Elspie grinned. "Well, thank you for picking him up."

Marsh kissed Sydney's cheek and then they all made their way into the club. Dinner was much more low-key than they'd experienced before. Sydney snuggled against Thane as the four of them had a quiet dinner and headed back to the apartment.

The rest of the evening was spent watching a movie and then Sydney crawled into bed with Thane, falling asleep safely tucked against him.

* * *

"Kade?" Samantha called, and waddled into the library, her hands resting on her enormous belly. After delivering Pepper's baby, the family had returned to Inverness to prep for the party. Gillian had also traveled with them so she'd be close.

"Aye, love," he said, and left his desk to wrap an arm around her. "Are you okay?"

She rubbed her belly. "Just some twangs."

"You should rest." Kade laid his hands over hers. "In case he comes."

"He's not coming yet." Samantha smiled. "He wouldn't dare."

Kade chuckled. "Sweetheart, all of this happened with Liam."

"No, it's a little different," she countered. "Besides, I've had a conversation with our wee Phineas and told him he has to wait until after the party."

"Which is in a week," Kade pointed out. "I think he's coming tonight."

She shook her head. "But I have too much to do."

"And it will all get done, love." He wrapped his arms around her. "You have a family who can help you, and your parents get here tomorrow."

She dropped her head on his chest and took a deep breath. "Kade?"

"Yes, love."

"My water just broke."

"I know." He bent down and lifted her in his arms, carrying her out of the library and up to their bedroom. Once he settled her on the bed, he called for his staff and then dialed Gillian's number.

"She's laboring?" Gillian asked.

"Aye. Her water broke six minutes ago."

"I'll be there soon."

"Thank you."

Gillian hung up and Kade made his way back to Samantha. "Let's get you out of those clothes, love."

Bearnas, the head maid, knocked on the door and entered when bid. "I have sheets, milord."

"Thank you," he said, and wrapped his arms around Samantha. "Up, love."

She slid off the bed and looped her arms around his neck, dropping her head on his chest and taking a few deep breaths. "I feel him, baby. He's coming."

Kade felt her contraction and took as much pain as he could while Bearnas got the bed ready. Gillian fluttered in less than five minutes later and helped Kade get Samantha on the bed, just as she begged to push. Pepper arrived less than a minute before Phineas's head crowned and grabbed Samantha's hand, kissing her cheek. "I'm so proud of you."

"Nice of you to show up," Samantha retorted, and then let out a groan as she pushed.

Pepper grinned. "I'm always right on time."

Phineas Dalton James Gunnach arrived ten minutes later, nine pounds, six ounces and twenty-two inches long. He had a full head of blond hair and cried for about a minute before Samantha settled him to her breast and he latched on like a pro. "He's perfect," Kade whispered, and kissed his mate and new son.

Samantha stroked his head. "My wee Finn. He looks just like Li—"

"Sam?" Kade's heart raced as he felt her lose her grasp with consciousness.

"She's bleeding quite heavily, your majesty," Gillian said.

Pepper took Finn from Samantha just as her arms went limp.

"Shite." Kade jumped off the bed, gently as to not jostle Samantha and then laid his hands on her stomach.

"I need to get a bit of this bleeding under control first, milord," Gillian said. "Then you can heal her."

The waiting was torture as Gillian worked to get Samantha to a place Kade could do some good.

"All right, milord. She's ready," Gillian said.

Pepper laid a hand on Samantha's shoulder as she cradled Finn and Kade did the final healing, doing only what a mate could do. It took longer than he felt should be normal before she started to come around. He kept his hands on her even as she blinked her eyes open. "What happened?" she asked, and frowned. "What's wrong?"

"Don't move, love," Kade demanded. "There was a complication."

Samantha reached for Finn. "Give me the baby."

Pepper nodded and laid him in Samantha's arms. Samantha settled him at her breast again.

"I'll check again, milord," Gillian said, and Kade gave her some space.

"What's going on?"

"You hemorrhaged, milady. It appears the bleeding has stopped now, but we'll watch you for the next few hours."

"I'm okay, honey." Samantha reached for Kade. "The baby's okay."

Kade took her hand, but couldn't relax.

"Kade," Samantha pressed. "Come and see your son."

"She's fine, milord," Gillian said. "It's all right."

Kade settled beside Samantha again and kissed her gently. "I'm so proud of you, love."

She smiled. "This was nothin'."

He chuckled and kissed his son's head. "You scared the shite out of me."

"Don't cuss in front of the baby."

He rolled his eyes. "Aye, love."

If Samantha was being bossy, she was feeling better. This relieved him more than anything.

Pepper slipped out of the room, returning a few minutes later with Liam. "Someone wants to meet his brother."

"Mama," he called.

"Come here, baby," Samantha said, and Pepper settled him beside her.

"Gently, Liam," Kade said.

"Aye, Da," he whispered. "Baby."

"Yes, baby." Samantha smiled. "Phineas."

Liam gave a toothy grin. "Baby."

"Yes, baby." Samantha giggled. "I don't know if I'll get used to how advanced our babies are compared to human babies."

"It is weird to have them speaking in complete sentences at barely a year old," Pepper agreed.

"I didn't realize this was strange," Kade said, giving Liam a goofy grin.

"Not strange, but certainly unique," Sam said.

"LiLi, are you hungry?" Pepper asked.

He nodded and raised his arms for his auntie to pick him up.

"Cody and Chelsea are downstairs with Uncle Con. We'll go get some dinner, okay?"

Liam cupped her face and smiled. "'K, Peppy."

Pepper kissed him. "You are going to be heartbreaker."

"He already is," Samantha complained.

Pepper grinned, leaning down to kiss her cheek. "Well done, Mama."

"Thanks, Pep. Love you."

"Love you too. You rest. We'll take care of the kids. Payton and Brodie are on their way."

Kade rose to his feet and kissed Liam's cheek, then Pepper's. "Thanks, love."

"Anytime."

"I'll come with you," Gillian said. "I'll be here if you need me, milord."

"Thank you, Gillian."

Pepper and Gillian left the room and Kade settled in for a watchful night. Regardless of the scare earlier, Samantha appeared to be fine now. Kade couldn't feel anything off in her body so he held his wife and they got acquainted with their new son.

CHAPTER FOURTEEN

THANE HUNG UP the phone and walked into the kitchen where Sydney was cooking dinner.

"Everything okay?" she asked.

He smiled. "The king and queen have a new wee son. He was almost two weeks early."

"Oh wow. How are they doing?"

"Very well."

"Elspie said that when there's a familial bond, the women often deliver around the same time." Sydney raised an eyebrow. "Maybe we should postpone going early."

"Sam still wants us to come tomorrow," Thane said. "And apparently, Liam's birthday is going on as planned, so we're all still invited."

"She's up to a party already?"

Thane nodded. "Gestation for Cauld Ane women is six months, love, and healing is immediate, so she's doing very well."

"Six months?" she squeaked.

"Aye, love." Thane chuckled. "Does that frighten you?"

She shook her head. "Not when it's happening to someone else."

He wrapped his arms around her from behind and kissed her neck. "There's no rush, sweetheart. We'll wait until you're ready."

"I appreciate that." She sighed. "Big time."

"Do you want children?"

She turned in his arms and looped them around his neck. "With you? Yes. Hundreds."

He laughed. "Hundreds?"

"Okay, at least two... or four."

Thane kissed her. "Four will be good."

"Or maybe five."

"However many you want to give me, love." He kissed her again. "I'll be happy."

"This is my decision, then?"

"Considering you have to do all the heavy lifting... yes."

Sydney smiled and ran her fingers through his hair. "Well, we'll have one and then see where we go from there."

"Sounds good." He kissed her again and then patted her on the bottom. "Want some wine?"

"Yes, please. Dinner's almost done."

"Your cousin said your meatballs are 'to die for.'" He did his best imitation of Lucy and Sydney laughed.

"I absolutely see why you get paid the big bucks for acting."

He gave her a theater bow. "Thank you, milady."

"It doesn't get you out of chores, however. Set the table, mister movie star and we'll eat."

"Where are my people?" He snapped a finger in the air. "Staff? Staff? Where are you?"

Sydney dissolved into giggles. "You are ridiculous."

* * *

The next afternoon after flying first class into Inverness, Sydney and Thane slid into the SUV the king had sent to bring them to his home. The drive from the airport through the Scottish countryside was breathtaking and Sydney found herself constantly oohing and aahing the further into the wilderness they drove.

"We're almost there," Thane said, and took her hand. "Just over this ridge."

Sydney couldn't keep her mouth closed as they crossed the drawbridge and pulled into a large courtyard. It was like a little city within the remote country setting with people milling around, she assumed preparing for the guests who would arrive in a week.

The car was met by very official gentlemen in kilts, and one opened her door while the other opened Thane's. "We'll get your bags, sir," the man closest to Thane said.

Thane nodded and held his hand out to Sydney. She took it and they made their way to the front door. It opened before they could ring the bell and Thane smiled. "Good day, Mr. Winston."

"Mr. Allen, welcome. Miss Warren."

Sydney smiled. "Hi."

She was surprised he knew her name.

He's prepared for everything, love.

They were ushered into a roomy foyer and then into the great hall. Sydney tried not to look overly awed, but she couldn't help it. It was magnificent. Three stories high, with balconies peering down from the top floors, the ceiling came to a large arch with a wooden beam running the length of the room, holding six chandeliers.

The fireplace was almost as tall as it was wide, and looked like it could fit several large men, and it was lit, not that it warmed the large space. The room was set up in sections. A massive table was off to the left, with tall chairs surrounding it.

To the right was a sitting area in front of the fire. Three sofas and two overstuffed chairs surrounded a coffee table that looked rather modern in the historical home. The third section housed a piano, with folding chairs propped against the wall.

"You made it!" A woman with long brown hair carrying a swaddled bundle came walking towards them.

Thane bowed. "Majesty."

"Oh, stop!" she demanded. "I'm going to get enough of that nonsense next week."

Thane chuckled. "Samantha, may I present my mate, Sydney. Sweetheart, this is Her Majesty, Queen Samantha."

Samantha sighed. "Seriously?"

Thane laughed. "Sorry, couldn't resist."

"Call me Samantha, or better yet, Sam," she said. "*Please.*"

Sydney smiled. "It's wonderful to meet you, Samantha. Is this Phineas?"

"Yes." Samantha turned him so they could get a better look. "He's finally sleeping."

"We should probably whisper, then," Sydney suggested, but Samantha shook her head.

"He needs to learn to sleep through the noise. It's what we did with Liam and he'll sleep anywhere now."

"Smart," Sydney said.

An older woman walked into the room and held her arms out. "Shall I put him down, Majesty?"

"Yes, Bearnas, thank you." She handed the baby off and then hugged Thane and Sydney. "Come on, I'll show you to your room. I hope you don't mind, but I've put you in together. I figured since tomorrow's your bonding night, it means you don't have to move."

"That's perfect, Sam, thank you," Thane said.

They followed Samantha up the staircase to the left of the foyer and to the third door down. She pushed open the door and stepped inside, and Thane guided Sydney in front of him.

A large bed with ornately carved posts held a canopy draped in dark red velvet. Also in the room was a dresser and two high-backed chairs that faced a small fireplace, sitting between two large windows. Their bags sat at the end of the bed waiting for them to unpack.

"You have a bathroom right through that door." Samantha pointed to the door beside the bed. "And your closet has another bureau. Please make yourselves at home. We aren't formal here... well, we aren't right now." She giggled. "The party will be a little different."

"It's going to be great," Thane said.

"I think so, too." Samantha smiled. "Dinner's at six and we won't dress up. Just come as you are. I have to feed the baby, but come downstairs when you're settled and we'll have some wine before dinner."

"Thanks for everything," Sydney said.

Samantha squeezed her hand. "You're so welcome, Sydney. Don't worry about tomorrow night. I promise, it's going to be great."

Sydney nodded as she leaned against Thane.

"I'll see you in a few."

Sam left and Sydney wrapped her arms around Thane. "This room is unreal."

He smiled. "Aye, lass, 'tis."

"And this is where it'll happen?"

Thane gave her a gentle squeeze. "If you feel comfortable, aye. If not, we can go somewhere else."

"I feel great, honey. I wish we could do this tonight."

"We can at midnight if you want to."

"Oh, I don't want to put anyone out," Sydney said.

"We won't be putting anyone out," he said, and kissed her forehead.

She leaned back. "Honey, this isn't our home, you can't just wave your movie star card and demand they do what you say."

Thane grinned. "What's this nonsense you're saying, milady? All must kowtow to me."

Sydney giggled. "Hm-mm, you feel free to believe that. Quietly. In your mind, so only I hear it."

He laughed and leaned down to kiss her. "All right, love, we'll wait."

"Thank you."

"Shall we unpack and then head downstairs?"

Sydney nodded. "Perfect."

As they were unpacking, Sydney's phone rang and she smiled as she answered it. "Hey, Luce."

"Hey. How's the trip going?"

"So far, so good. Miss me?"

Lucy giggled. "So, so bad. Especially because you're missing all the drama."

"Uh-oh, what drama?"

"Zach's just being a dick. He's sending threatening texts and leaving dead flowers on my car and stuff."

"Why would he do that?"

"I have no idea, but Dad's team is on it, so I'm not worried. It's just that now security's tightened, which means, no fun for Lucy."

Sydney hummed sympathetically. "I'm sorry, cuz. Next time, you'll just have to come with us. You'd love it up here."

"You're on. For now, though, Mum's calling, so I better go. Send me some photos, would you?"

"Of course."

"Love you, Sid."

"Love you too, Luce." Sydney hung up and went back to her unpacking.

* * *

Sydney followed Thane downstairs and into the great hall. Pepper pushed herself out of her seat, holding baby Chelsea close to her breast, and pulled Sydney in for a hug. "Welcome."

"Hi," Sydney said, and hugged her.

"Careful, love," Connall ordered.

"Bite me, honey," Pepper retorted, and her mate chuckled, but still watched her closely. "He's extra protective of this little one. Dating's going to be a nightmare."

"We don't date, love. Remember that."

Pepper smiled. "Her bonding night's going to be a nightmare."

"Och, Pepper, no bonding in regards to our daughter," Connall demanded.

"See?"

Sydney giggled and kissed the baby's head. "She's beautiful."

"Thank you."

Sydney and Thane greeted the rest of the family and she found herself a little intimidated by Kade. It might have been because she knew he was a king, but it was also his countenance. He was regal and hovered over his wife like any overprotective man would.

Thane kissed her temple. *We all hover, love. Don't let it scare you.*

She gave him a barely perceptible nod.

"Do you want some wine, Sydney?" Samantha asked.

"I would love some," she said as she sat beside Thane on one of the love seats.

"Red or white?"

"Red, please."

A glass of red appeared before her on a tray held by a young woman in uniform.

"Thank you," Sydney said, smiling at her.

"So," Samantha said. "We were wondering how you might feel about bonding at midnight."

Sydney glanced at Thane and he raised his hands in surrender. "I said nothing, love."

She narrowed her eyes.

"Seriously. I've been with you all day. When would I have?"

Samantha giggled. "I take it this subject came up?"

"Aye," Thane said. "Sydney didn't want to put anyone out."

"Oh, it's fine, Sydney," Samantha assured her. "We don't go to sleep early when we're here, so if you want to bond as soon as your birthday's official, please feel free to."

"We'll talk about it," Thane said. "Okay, love?"

Sydney nodded, forcing her nerves down.

It'll be fine, sweetheart.

She nodded again. "We'll talk about it," she parroted.

"You let me know what you want to do and we'll organize the staff."

"Thank you, Samantha," Sydney said.

"No problem."

"We'll all be here," Pepper added. "So, you have nothing to worry about."

"Aye, Sydney," Payton said. "We're here for you."

"I appreciate it."

Thane linked his fingers with hers and lifted her hand to his lips.

The rest of the evening went by in a blur of sorts. Sydney couldn't really focus on much, as her mind was preoccupied by the fact that in a few short hours, she would be permanently bound to the man who stayed glued to her the entire night. She wasn't nervous, although, she wondered if she should be. Everything was happening very quickly.

CHAPTER FIFTEEN

At eleven forty-five, Thane pulled her aside and gave her a sweet kiss. "Do you want to go up and I'll join you shortly?"

Sydney nodded.

"Are you all right, love?" he asked, and stroked her cheek. "We can wait."

"I don't want to wait, Thane." She smiled. "I'm excited. It's just a little overwhelming."

"I know." He squeezed her hand. "I'll see you in a little bit."

Sydney walked up to their room and found the lingerie she'd packed for their special night. After changing, she stepped into the bathroom to brush out her hair and clean her teeth. She heard the bedroom door click shut and walked out of the bathroom to find Thane pulling off his shirt.

Sydney leaned against the doorframe and watched him. He caught sight of her and his eyes swept her body. "Shite, love."

She giggled. "Do you approve?"

"Aye. You're stunning."

"So are you." She moved further into the room. "Now what?"

Thane smiled. "First, I'm going to kiss you, because I have to."

She snapped her fingers. "Well, hustle on over here, then."

He closed the distance between them and covered her mouth with his. She couldn't help herself from sliding her hand up his chest, breaking the kiss and sighing. "You're ridiculously gorgeous, Thane Allen."

"Yeah?"

"Yeah."

The little clock on the fireplace mantel chimed twelve times and he cupped her cheek. "Do you want wine first or do you want to start?"

"I want to start."

"Me too," he said. "Okay, repeat after me. *Ég gef þér allt sem ég er, allt sem ég vil vera og allt sem ég get verið.*"

"Oh, that's easy," she droned sarcastically.

"I'll think it as we go, so pull the words from my mind," he suggested. "Ready?"

Sydney nodded.

"Ég gef þér allt sem ég er, allt sem ég vil vera og allt sem ég get verið."

"Ég gef þér allt sem ég er, allt sem ég vil vera og allt sem ég get verið." Sydney felt her knees buckle and she grabbed for Thane.

He wrapped an arm around her waist. "I've got you, sweetheart."

"Okay." Sydney raised her arms and linked her fingers behind his neck.

"Ég er þin að eilífu. Skuldabréf okkar mun aldrei vera brotinn."

"Ég er þin að eilífu. Skuldabréf okkar mun aldrei vera brotinn." Sydney held onto his neck a little harder.

"I won't let you fall, love," Thane promised. "It's part of the bonding. Ready?" At her nod, he continued, "*Ást mín er alger.*"

"Ást mín er alger."

Thane lifted her before she could fall, and carried her to the bed. After he removed the rest of his clothing, he climbed onto the bed beside her and pulled her into his arms. "I give you everything I am, all I want to be, and all I can be. I'm yours forever. Our bond will never be broken. My love is absolute." He was gentle and attentive as he made love to her and she relished in the feeling of her body reaching for him of its own accord.

"That was amazing," she breathed out as they lay in bed and caught their breath.

He smiled, kissing her gently. "I love you."

"I love you, too." She kissed his chest. "What happens now?"

Thane chuckled. "We wait."

"I don't like to wait."

"What?" he asked in mock surprise. "I had no idea."

She laughed and smacked his chest gently. "I just want all this over with."

"I get it, love."

"Sorry, that's not very romantical is it?"

"Romantical?"

Sydney grinned. "Something my mom always said."

"I love it."

"She hated anything to do with schmultz. It was about the only thing we disagreed on. Anytime I wanted to watch a movie, she'd say, "It's not one of those romantical ones, is it?" It just kind of stuck." Sydney smiled, realizing her pain wasn't quite as heavy as she talked about her mom.

"I'm glad, love."

"You can still read my mind, I see."

Thane chuckled. "You were hoping for a different result?"

Before she could respond, hot fire shot through her legs and she cried out in agony.

"All right, love, it's starting. It's okay, I've got you."

The pain shifted to her feet and she whimpered, but she never got the chance to get used to the pain, because it moved to her left breast. This time she screamed. "I can't do this," she panted. "I can't."

Thane kept hold of her hand as he slid from the bed. "You can, sweetheart, I promise."

The fire licked at her stomach and then headed straight for her skull. Sydney groaned, trying to grab for her head, but Thane wouldn't let her. "Thane!"

"I have to stay connected to you," he said, and reached for his phone. "It's the only way I can alleviate any of your pain." With one hand, he grabbed a pair of sweats and tugged them on, then called Samantha.

Sydney couldn't focus on anything Thane was doing as the pain raged on in her body. Everything was on fire. "Thane," she rasped.

He squeezed her hand. "I know, sweetheart. Sam's on her way. It won't be long."

"I'm so hot."

"Okay, love. We're going to help."

* * *

A knock came at the door and Samantha slid in quietly, followed by Bearnas. The maid headed straight to the bathroom and Thane heard the water in the tub start. Another maid arrived with a bucket and also headed into the bathroom. Kade and Samantha had ice machines installed in each of the bathrooms, which helped with convenience, particularly in a situation like this. The Cauld Ane rarely got sick, but if they did, ice always helped to heal what ailed them.

"Pepper's coming with ice sheets," Samantha whispered, and made her way to Sydney's side. "I'm going to take your pulse, Sydney. You'll feel my fingers on your wrist, okay?"

Okay.

Thane smiled at Samantha. "She's ready."

Samantha grasped Sydney's wrist and Sydney let out a hiss of pain. "Take it from her, Thane," Samantha directed. "You're not focusing."

Thane nodded and concentrated on Sydney. She relaxed in stages as he kissed her palm.

"Good, Thane," Sam said. "Her pulse is slowing."

"The bath is ready, majesty," Bearnas said.

Samantha smiled at Sydney. "Thane's going to carry you into the bathroom, Sydney. It might hurt a bit, but the ice will help."

Sydney licked her lips. "I don't like the cold."

"You will now." Samantha squeezed her hand. "I promise."

At Samantha's nod, Thane lifted Sydney off the bed, trying to ignore her whimper as he carried her into the bathroom and lowered her into the ice water. Sydney let out a sigh and then opened her eyes. "Better. Thank you."

"Good, love."

"Can I please have some water?"

"I'll get it," Samantha said, and grabbed a glass, filling it from the tub and handing it to her.

Sydney gulped it down, choking a little as she drank.

"Slow down, love," Thane ordered.

"I'm so thirsty."

"That's normal, Sydney," Samantha said. "As soon as the worst is over, I'll set up a drip to rehydrate you."

"Can I have some more water, please?" she pleaded.

"Yes, of course." Samantha filled the glass again. This time Sydney sipped a little slower.

Thane's heart raced as he watched Sydney's body burn red. She cried out again as the glass slipped from her fingers, but he caught it before it shattered against the porcelain tub. "Shite! What's happening to her?"

"Her body's expelling her human elements. It's okay, Thane. We just need to cool the water. Don't lose touch." Samantha reached in and pulled the stopper, letting a little water escape while Bearnas began to dump buckets of ice into the water. Samantha secured the tub again and then took the glass from Thane and refilled it.

Thane knelt on the floor and kissed Sydney's hand gently. "I'm here, love. I won't let go."

She smiled and turned her head toward him, but didn't open her eyes. "I'm okay, honey. It's better now."

Thane frowned up at Samantha. "Can you give her something, Sam?"

"No, not yet. I'm sorry, Thane. I know this sucks, but her body just needs to do its thing." She squeezed his shoulder. "It's harder on you guys than it is on us, trust me."

"Speak for yourself," Sydney retorted, her eyes still closed, but her body back to its normal color and temperature.

Samantha smiled. "See? The snark's a good sign."

Thane settled his free hand on Sydney's forehead. "Are you in pain, love?"

Sydney finally opened her eyes and squeezed his hand. "No, not pain. It's kind of like...I don't know?"

"Something tickling your skin?" Samantha asked.

"Yes, exactly! I'm on the verge of itchy, but not like I need to scratch."

"Good," Samantha said. "We'll get the bed ready. You'll sleep in ice sheets for a few hours and then you'll be a little groggy tomorrow, but you've actually come through this faster than most of us."

"I have?"

Samantha smiled. "You have."

"That's because she's a star," Thane said.

"Takes one to know one," Samantha said, and left the bathroom.

Sydney giggled. It was the best thing Thane had heard all day. Her laugh settled in his soul and drove away the gut wrenching fear he'd been feeling for the last hour.

"I'm okay, honey," Sydney whispered, releasing his hand so she could cup his face. He grasped her arm, afraid to let any distance come between them.

"Is the pain okay?" he asked.

Sydney smiled. "Yep. I actually feel really good. Just a little sleepy."

"Thane?" Samantha called from the bedroom.

"Aye?"

"If the pain's done, you can help Sydney dry off so she can sleep."

"All right." He smiled at his mate and kissed her palm. "You ready to get out before you prune?"

"You have a problem with prunes?"

He kissed her gently. "I love prunes, particularly if my mate happens to be one of them."

"Look who's all romantical now," she quipped.

Thane grinned, pulling the plug on the tub and grabbing a towel. He helped Sydney to her feet and wrapped an arm around her waist to keep her anchored while she climbed out. After drying her off gently, he secured the towel around her and carried her back to the bed.

"I'm so thirsty," Sydney rasped as he pulled the sheets over her body.

"I have a saline drip for you, Sydney," Samantha said. "It'll help." She slid the needle effortlessly into Sydney's arm and taped it off before hanging the bag on a hook by the bed. "I wish we'd had this when Kade bound me. Pepper could have used one too. We just didn't know how our bodies would react to anything, but we've been finding things out as we go."

"Thanks for everything, Sam," Sydney said with a sleepy smile. "I can't imagine having gone through this without help."

"I know, hon," she said, and squeezed her arm. "It was terrifying for Kade more than me, so I promised I wouldn't let any more of our people deal with this."

"Not for you?" she asked.

Samantha giggled. "Not like it was for him, no. Neither of us knew what was happening, because his parents had held back a lot of information about their...ah, our race. It was a nightmare for Kade. He thought I was dying." She closed her eyes and then smiled. "Sorry, he's arguing with me now as we speak."

Sydney chuckled. "I have no idea what that's like on any level."

Cheeky.

"Like right now," she retorted.

Thane smiled and shook his head.

"Okay, I'm going to feed my newest munchkin." Sam checked the fluids bag and then Sydney's pulse. "I'll check in on you in an hour and if you're feeling good, we'll take that pesky needle out of your arm. If you need anything in the meantime, ring the bell. Bearnas will either know what to do or find me."

"Thanks for everything, Sam." Thane hugged her, giving her a gentle kiss on her cheek.

"If I'd known all I had to do was take care of a friend to get some affection from a big movie star, I would have done that earlier." She giggled. "Hush, Kade."

Thane wasn't sure if she was aware she'd said that out loud, but he didn't mention it, and Samantha left them alone. After getting another glass of water for Sydney, he climbed into bed beside her, pulling her gently into his arms. "I love you, sweetheart."

She sighed and kissed him gently. "I love you, too."

"Sleep now."

And she did.

* * *

Sydney felt a small tug on her arm and opened her eyes to find Samantha pulling the needle out. "Sorry, hon. I didn't mean to wake you."

"No, that's okay."

"I figured you'd feel better if you could move a bit."

Sydney smiled and bit back a yawn. "Where's Thane?"

"He's just getting fresh ice sheets." Samantha took her pulse again and then checked her temperature. "Your temperature's rising a little again."

Sydney sat up a little. "Is that bad?"

"I don't think so. It's just not something we've seen before. I'm going to get another drip in case. But I'll wait until Thane gets back."

"Okay," Sydney whispered, unable to keep her eyes open.

"Sydney?"

"Hmm?"

"Sid?" Samantha said, her tone urgent.

Sydney couldn't concentrate and then the burning started again and she heard herself cry out.

* * *

Thane heard Sydney's cry and rushed back into the bedroom, dropping his burdens as he let out a bellow of rage. "What the hell is going on?"

Sydney was on the floor in the fetal position, shaking violently as she vomited into a bowl while Samantha and Bearnas packed her with ice.

"It's all right, Thane," Samantha assured. "This is all part of it. She just started a little later than the rest of us, so I'd kind of hoped she'd skipped it."

Thane knelt beside Sydney and laid his hand on her head, soaked with sweat. "Shite."

"I know it's frightening," Samantha said. "But this is all normal. It's okay. She'll be okay."

"I've got a new bath, Majesty," Bearnas said as she walked into the room.

"Thank you," Samantha said, and focused back on Thane. "In a minute, I'm going to need you to lift her again and take her into the bathroom."

Thane wasn't listening. He was trying to keep Sydney from choking on her hair. It was plastered around her face and he was trying to slide it away from her mouth. A small but strong hand grabbed his arm and he was forced to look at Samantha.

"Did you hear me?"

"What? No, sorry, I didn't," he confessed.

"When this is done, I'm going to need you to carry her back to the tub."

"Aye, lass. When this is done." He focused back on Sydney, stroking her hair.

I'm dying

You're not dying, love.

She let out a broken sigh. *I'm totally dying.*

He tried not to smile, but lost the battle. Even in pain, she was trying to make him feel better. "As soon as you're ready, I'm going to lift you, okay?"

No. There's no point. I'll be dead.

He stroked her cheek and her shaking calmed. "I'm here, baby."

She pushed up just enough to lay her head in his lap. *I feel like my body weighs a million trillion pounds.*

That's a lot in kilos.

It's a lot in pounds too. Sydney gave him a slight smile as she glanced down her body. "I have a weird mark on my knee."

"It's my mark," he explained.

Her eyes closed. *What do you mean?*

"I have the mark on my left knee. Now that we're bound, you have the one on your right."

"Is that normal?" she whispered.

"Aye, love, it's normal." Thane squeezed her hand. "I'm going to lift you now."

One more minute. She took a ragged breath. *I just need a little more time to enjoy no pain.*

"We're ready," Samantha said. "But take your time."

How's your stomach?

"It's better I think," she whispered.

"I'm going to lift you now," Thane said. "Arms around my neck, sweetheart."

She did as he instructed and he wrapped the ice sheet around her to keep her covered. Holding her close, he carried her into the bathroom and settled her into the water again. She let out a deep sigh and slid all the way under the water before sitting up with a smile. "Oh my word, this is awesome."

Thane sat on the edge of the tub and took her hand again, glancing up at Samantha. "Do you think it's over now?"

Samantha nodded. "It should be. Vomiting is typically the last thing to happen. It's interesting she slept for so long between. Her conversion was actually a lot less violent than some. It's a good sign."

Sydney squeezed Thane's hand. "I'm okay, honey."

He leaned down to kiss her but she turned her head.

He frowned. "Hey."

"I haven't brushed my teeth."

Thane grinned. "You don't need to now that you're Cauld Ane."

She frowned. "Seriously?"

"It's a definite perk," Samantha said. "That and being able to heal yourself and your family."

"I can do that?"

Thane nodded.

"What if I'm stabbed...or shot?"

Thane scowled. "You won't be stabbed or shot."

"But if you were," Samantha rushed to say. "You could heal yourself."

"Damn it, Sydney," Thane said.

"Just checking." Sydney gave him a slight smile as she ran her tongue over her teeth. "My teeth *do* feel clean."

Thane chuckled. "I'd like that kiss now, love."

She raised her head and obliged.

CHAPTER SIXTEEN

SYDNEY AWOKE TO darkness, her body pressed up against the warmth of her mate. She shifted and felt Thane's strong hand grip her thigh. "You keep moving yer bum against me, love, I won't be able to remain the gentleman."

Sydney giggled and rolled to face him. "I didn't marry you... ah, I mean, bond with you because you're a gentleman."

"No?"

She shook her head. "I bonded with you so you could show me a good time... debauchery and all."

He gripped her waist and rolled with her so she was straddling his hips. "Before I show you the true depth of my debaucheries, how are you feeling?"

"Amazing." Sydney leaned down and kissed his chest. "My body feels healthier than it's ever been."

"Yeah?"

"Yeah." She grinned. "I think we need to practice making a baby."

Thane laughed. "Already?"

"Hell, yes."

He flipped her onto her back. "Okay, love, we'll go slow so that I can teach you everything I know."

"What happens when the student becomes the master?"

Thane kissed her neck. "Then the fun really begins."

He made love to her and then it was time for their bonding ceremony. The official "marriage" for the purpose of Cauld Ane recordkeeping.

Thane had surprised her with a new dress to commemorate the occasion. A lace, off-white cocktail dress that settled a few inches above her knees. It had one shoulder and a wide satin sash and, with a pair of matching Jimmy Choo stilettos, she felt like a modern day princess. Thane pulled her into his arms and kissed her. "You are beautiful."

"So are you." He wore his traditional tartan kilt, the green and blues exceptional against his coloring.

"You're missing something," he said.

"I am?"

He grinned and pulled out a small, black, velvet box.

"What's this?" she asked, and gasped when he pried it open. A pair of white gold diamond teardrop earrings sparkled in the black satin. "Thane," she breathed out.

"Do you like them?"

She smiled. "Honey, they're exquisite."

"I have to admit, I wanted to buy the six-carat ones, but I know you enough to know that you'd feel uncomfortable wearing them."

"You're right." Sydney stroked his cheek. "I would. But these? These I can wear almost every day." She secured them to her ears.

Thane ran his thumb gently over one. "Perfect."

"Thank you, honey." She squeezed his hand. "I have something for you too."

"Something other than the red lacy gift I tore off your body last night?"

She giggled and pulled open the bureau drawer. "Yes."

Pulling out the gift bag with the statue, she handed it to him. "That's not all," she said, and stepped into the closet, sliding the real gift out of the front pocket of her tote. She walked back into the bedroom and pointed to the gift bag. "Open that first and then you can have this."

He raised an eyebrow and peeked into the bag, letting out a laugh that made Sydney grin. He pulled out the Oscar and studied it. "This is the best gift I've ever received."

"It's a major award, honey, and you earned it."

He leaned down and kissed her. "I love it. Almost as much as I love you."

She smiled and handed him the leather box, unwrapped. "Elspie helped me pick this out."

He set the Oscar on the dresser and took the box, opening it and shaking his head. "Baby."

"Is it okay? Do you like it?" She'd had the timepiece engraved and now she wasn't sure about it.

He pulled the watch out and kissed her again. "It's amazing, love. Even better than the Oscar."

"Wow, that's high praise. I won't tell the Academy."

Thane turned it over and read the back. "*I'm blessed to call you mine. All my love, Mrs. Movie Star.*" He smiled. "I'm the blessed one, Sydney. I love you."

"I love you too." He kissed her, sliding her dress up over her hips. "Thane, you'll ruin the dress."

"I'll be very, very careful."

"Even if you are, honey, we don't have time."

"I'll make it quick."

"You haven't made it quick yet."

"I will now," he promised, and kept his word.

After putting themselves back together, Sydney followed Thane downstairs and into the throne room. She was shocked to find his entire family in attendance. Even though they'd discussed the option for her to invite hers, she'd decided that she wanted to experience the traditional ceremony, rather than one that was "human sensitive."

Thane had promised a wedding to rival all weddings once the situation with her mother was sorted, so she was happy to keep their bonding between them for the moment. But her heart swelled when they joined the pastor and Thane's family was there, along with their closest friends.

Isolde wrapped Sydney in a warm embrace and kissed her cheek. "You look stunning, love."

"Thank you."

Domnall was next and his gruff, but no less warm, hug brought tears to Sydney's eyes. "You're the best of who we could have imagined for him, lass. A gift from God."

"Thank you," she rasped.

It took several more minutes to hug each of the rest of the family and then it was time to start the ceremony.

As the group settled in their seats, Thane and Sydney faced each other and Pastor Kent smiled at them and then the congregation. "Thane and Sydney have chosen a traditional hand fasting until they can join together in human matrimony. I am to understand you have bonded?"

"Aye, pastor," Thane said.

"I'm happy for you both." He reached for the Allen tartan ribbon and studied each of them. "Join your right hands."

Sydney giggled when she nearly raised her left, but recovered quickly and clasped Thane's hand.

"May the best you've ever seen be the worst you'll ever see." Pastor Kent bound the ribbon around their hands as he recited the ancient Scottish blessing. "May the mouse never leave your pantry with a teardrop in his eye. May you always keep healthy and hearty until you're old enough to die. May you always be just as happy as we wish you now to be. You may now kiss your mate."

Using their joined hands as leverage, Thane tugged Sydney to him and kissed her deeply. Domnall hollered and pulled Thane away from Sydney, causing the guests to laugh...she, however, blushed beet red.

Domnall untied their hands and they signed the royal book, then it was time to party, which they did until the wee hours.

* * *

The next morning, Thane drove Sydney down to the stables and they mounted a couple of horses to ride over to Max and Grace's home, just a few miles from the castle.

Sydney was a little nervous to hang out with the famous rock star, but it helped that Niall and Charlotte would be there as well. It was one thing to shake the man's hand, and an entirely different one to spend a morning with him. Arriving at the expansive white mansion, Sydney did her best to take it all in. Ivy wove its way up one side of the house, adding to the historical façade, while the cobblestone courtyard offered the perfect welcome that led to the blue seven-foot-tall, six-foot-wide double doors at the front.

Thane's hand on her leg drew her focus to him as he stood below her and she smiled down at him. "Mmm, I like this angle."

He chuckled. "Would you like me to stand here for a while?"

"I'd say yes, but then we'd be late to brunch." She giggled and slid her foot out of the stirrups, dismounting with the help of her very sexy man.

A groom walked the horses away, and Thane took Sydney's hand and led her to the front door.

Grace pulled the door open before they'd even reached the porch and hugged Sydney then Thane. "Welcome! I'm so glad you guys could make it."

A flurry of blonde slammed into Thane's legs. "Unca Thane!!" the little girl squealed.

Thane chuckled and lifted her into his arms. "Well, hello there, sweetpea."

"Moira!" Charlotte rushed out in an attempt to catch her. "Lordy, she's quick."

"It's the Cauld Ane in her," Thane said. "Sydney, this is Niall and Charlotte's daughter, the beautiful Moira Faith."

"Hi Moira, it's nice to meet you."

"Hi," she whispered, and dropped her head on Thane's shoulder.

"Come in," Grace said, and waved them inside.

Thane gave Moira a gentle hug and stepped back so Sydney could precede him into the house. Sydney was just as impressed by Grace and Max's home as she had been with the castle. Their home was laid out over three stories, with a library, kitchen, parlor, great room, dining room, bedroom, and two full bathrooms on the first floor. Six large bedrooms, each with their own bathroom, were on the second floor, as well as a large common room and an additional bathroom.

The third floor was considered the family's private quarters, with a gigantic master suite and four other bedrooms with private bathrooms. Elevators on each end of the home covered each story and the basement.

"It's ridiculously big, isn't it?" Grace murmured.

"I think it's beautiful," Sydney said.

"Thank you." Grace grinned. "Max had a little emergency with one of the horses, so he and Niall will be back in a bit. Make yourselves at home. Can I get you some wine or pop?"

"I'd love a beer if you have one, please," Thane said, and lowered Moira to the floor.

"Of course we have beer... we're not animals."

Thane laughed. "Thanks, lass."

"I'm happy with water for now," Sydney said.

"I'll be right back." Grace walked out of the room and Moira dragged Thane to the sofa.

"Book," she demanded, and handed him Cinderella.

"Moira, honey, let's give Uncle Thane a minute, huh?"

"She's fine, Charlotte." Thane pulled Moira onto his lap and Sydney sat next to them.

Thane got two lines into the book before Moira slid off his lap and made a run for Niall. "Daddy!"

"Ah, the fickleness of ladies," Thane said, and chuckled as he rose to his feet. Sydney followed suit.

"Famous drummer beats movie star, apparently," Sydney said.

Niall hugged Thane and then Sydney. Once Max had said hello, he went to help Grace. Charlotte sat beside Niall and Moira, but her phone rang and she sighed. "Sorry, I have to get this, it's Pepper."

"Don't worry on our account," Thane said, and wrapped an arm around Sydney, pulling her close.

Grace and Max walked in with drinks and then sat with Niall.

"How do you feel Sydney?" Grace asked.

"Great, actually."

"It's a little strange, huh?"

"Yeah, it is. My body feels different, but not so different I don't still feel like me."

Grace nodded. "Just wait until you find out you can lift three times your body weight."

"Is that a thing?"

Thane jostled her gently. "Yeah, baby, it's a thing."

"I want to do it now!"

He chuckled. "How about we do it later?"

Sydney wrinkled her nose. "You're no fun."

Charlotte returned and flopped down beside Niall.

"Everything okay?" he asked.

She smiled. "Yep. I just need to go early tomorrow to help set up."

"We were already going early."

"I'm aware. But apparently Pepper forgot." Charlotte sighed. "I'm giving her new-mother-brain-loss grace."

Grace giggled. "You'd think it was her party with how stressed out she's making herself."

Charlotte groaned. "No doubt."

"Well, we're staying there, so we can help as well," Sydney said.

"Oh, you will," Charlotte decreed.

Sydney giggled. "Just put us to work. Apparently, I can now lift heavy things, so my damsel in distress gig is over."

Thane kissed her temple. "You'll always be my wee damsel, love."

"I will?" she asked with a saccharin tone, clutching her hands to her chest. "You're the bestest most awesomest mate in the whole wide world."

"Damn straight." Thane laughed and kissed her.

The rest of the day was spent in comfortable ribbing and conversation. By the time they had to leave to go back to the castle, Sydney felt like she had lifelong friends.

Thane took her to bed that night and she was able to fall asleep without his help. She couldn't wait to find out what more her new body would do for her, but in the meantime, she was going to enjoy the hell out of what it was doing now.

* * *

Sydney's alarm buzzed her awake at seven the next morning. She hit the snooze and rolled over to snuggle close to Thane again.

"It's not morning, is it?" he groaned.

She smiled, kissing his chest. "Yep. 'Fraid so."

"I can't move," he complained. "I think you broke me last night."

Sydney laughed. "Just testing out my new limits. I know I don't have any point of reference, but sex is *awesome* in my new vessel."

Thane chuckled just as her alarm buzzed again and she pulled away to turn it off, sliding off the bed.

"Okay, mister movie star, time to get up. Come shower with me and I'll fix whatever ails you."

He jumped from the bed. "Don't have to tell me twice."

"You're a quick study, honey."

Thane laughed and smacked her bottom as he passed her. "Come on, baby. I'm dying to soap you up."

She shivered as she followed him into the bathroom.

Once showered and dressed, they headed down to the great hall and Sydney laughed as Samantha stood in the middle of the room directing traffic while she cradled Phineas in her arms.

"Wow, you're a pro," Sydney said.

Samantha smiled. "Oh, you missed me blubbering in the corner an hour ago when Kade had to talk me down off the ledge."

Sydney smiled sympathetically. "You could have canceled. No one would have faulted you."

"A Moore...ah, I mean a Gunnach, never gives up."

Samantha's maiden name, Thane provided.

Thane laughed. "Well, what can we do? Put us to work."

"Sydney, Grace and Charlotte are working on gift bags in the library, would you please help them with that?"

"Of course."

Samantha smiled. "And Thane, Max is setting up the sound and video stuff. If you wouldn't mind helping him with that, I'd appreciate it. He's in the garden."

"No problem."

"Eat first, though, okay?" Samantha rocked the baby when he fussed. "Breakfast is set out in the kitchen."

"Thanks, Sam," Thane said.

"No, thank you," she quipped.

Thane guided Sydney to the kitchen and then, once they ate, they split up to take care of their tasks.

* * *

Guests started trickling in at noon, dignitaries the first to arrive, and Sydney soon found out all of them were Cauld Ane. There would be humans in attendance, but they wouldn't arrive until four, which gave their people a chance to speak unhindered for a few hours.

"There are so many people," Sydney whispered as she grasped Thane's shirt before he could get away from her.

He chuckled, facing her and pulling her against his chest. "You're fine, love."

"Don't you dare leave me."

"I'm not leaving you, baby, I'm going to talk to Niall."

She threw her arms in the air. "That's leaving me... to go and talk to Niall."

He raised an eyebrow.

"What?" With a gasp, she squealed, "Thane," as he pinned her arms and lifted her off her feet, carrying her over to where Niall stood with Charlotte.

Oh my word, I'm going to kill you.

He laughed, setting her down again and kissing her soundly in front of everyone. Heat covered her neck and face and she stepped behind him in an effort to hide.

No one's watching us, love.

I don't believe you. She tugged on his shirt. *I need a second, but murder is still on the table.*

Is twerking off of it?

"Thane," she whispered dropping her forehead to his back.

"It's just us, love."

She peeked over his shoulder and felt her blush again as Charlotte and Niall watched her with smiles. Sydney shook her head and stepped behind him.

"It's a lot, huh?" Charlotte said.

"Sorry, I don't mean to be rude."

Charlotte giggled. "Don't be sorry, seriously. Why do you think we're hiding here in the corner? Niall would be out there yuckin' it up with pretty much everyone here if it wasn't for me."

Niall grinned. "I'm happy to be wherever you are, love."

Charlotte wrapped her arms around his bicep. "That's because you're a smart man."

Thane wrapped an arm around Sydney's waist and kissed her temple. "We can stay here for as long as you need."

"I'm not an invalid, Thane. I just feel a little overwhelmed."

"We *are* in a unique position where we can leave and hang out in the library if we'd like to," Niall said.

Charlotte gasped. "We can?"

"Aye, lass. We've said hello to everyone we need to. We don't have to come back out until four."

"Then why are we still here?"

"We're going right now," Thane said.

Sydney laughed. "Someone else who's proving to be smart."

Thane took her hand and gave it a squeeze, then the couples headed into the library. Sydney giggled when she found Pepper, Max, Grace, and Payton there. Samantha breezed in a few minutes later, Phineas in her arms. "If I'd known the party was in here, I would have escaped hours ago."

"I had to feed the baby," Pepper said, baby Chelsea cradled against her.

"What a coincidence, Phineas needs to be fed as well." Samantha sat in one of the overstuffed chairs and threw a blanket over her and Phineas to feed him.

See, love? You're in great company.

Sydney grinned up at him. *Yes, apparently I am.*

The rest of the evening was part meeting strangers and part connecting with new friends, including spending more time with Thane's family. Sydney couldn't imagine a better evening, and

Ainsley was ecstatic because she had been given permission to ride Max's horses the next day.

Midnight came faster than expected and Thane insisted on taking Sydney to bed. She didn't complain (much), as they made their way upstairs. And once he'd kissed every inch of her body, he made love to her and she realized how perfect their time at the castle had been.

In some ways, she didn't want it to end.

CHAPTER SEVENTEEN

THE NEXT DAY, Thane walked into the king's chapel and took his place in the Allen pew. His father was not there today like he normally would be for a council meeting, as Kade had only called together those who led high-profile lives.

This meant that all the members of Fallen Crown were in attendance, along with several other men and women who were known both locally, nationally, and internationally for different careers, the most surprising being Ewan McFadden, who had been voted Scotland's sexiest botanist. Somewhat random and funny, but it now put him into a category where he could no longer hide. All-in-all, there were close to sixty people in the room.

Kade and Samantha sat with Connall and Brodie and their mates, and Samantha smiled at Thane, her expression one of overwhelmed resignation. Anyone who knew her understood how uncomfortable she was at official gatherings, but she always handled them with grace and humor.

Niall slid in beside him even though it wasn't technically his family pew. "Hey."

Thane shook his hand. "You're a little late."

Niall chuckled. "Moira was having a hard time letting her da out the door."

"Not yer mate?"

"Sadly, no," Niall said. "Charlotte was trying to pry Moira the spider monkey from my body. I left her with my screaming daughter who you would think was never going to see me again."

Before Thane could comment, Kade walked to the middle of the dais. "Welcome everyone." The din died down as the king spoke. "I've asked you here because we need to discuss our public profiles going forward. All of you are high-profile, and depending on how long you plan to be high-profile, humans will start to notice that we don't age at the same rate as they do. About every fifty years, we face this dilemma and need to brainstorm how we want to handle it. Some of us may decide to go underground, out of the limelight; others may opt to cope another way."

"I vote to kill off Max in some tragic but messy accident," Connall said. "Fiery car crash should do it."

"I'm too damn pretty to go out in a fiery car crash," Max countered. "But I have a few ideas for you, brother. Guillotine is the immediate choice. I'll even have one built at my home if that will help expedite things."

The room erupted in laughs.

"We'll forget the feud between Max and Con for the moment," Kade said. "Especially considering that the fight has been going on for several hundred years and I see no end anytime soon." He waited for the laughs to die down again and raised his hands. "This meeting is a short one, to introduce the topic for our next meeting in the spring, when I hope you'll have some *legitimate*"—he glared at Connal and then at Max—"and effective ideas for how to handle this ongoing problem we have as Cauld Ane in a human world. In the spring we can discuss what your plans are and how we can support you. I'm sure I don't have to remind you not to put anything in writing. Thank you for your time."

The room stood en masse, bowed to Kane, and then filed out. Thane and Niall walked out together, while Max stayed behind to speak with Connall.

"I love it when these things are short," Thane confessed.

"Aye, brother. Me as well."

"How long are you staying?"

"We're leaving day after tomorrow. What about you?"

"Same, but we're heading back to London first."

"Grace and Charlotte want to know if you and Sydney want to join us for dinner tonight," Niall said, as he and Thane walked to the cars.

Do you want to have dinner with the MacMillan's tonight?

Sounds fun. Are you finished?

Aye, lass. Be home soon.

"We'd love to," Thane said.

"Perfect." Niall grinned. "Six?"

"We'll see you then," Thane said, and climbed into the car. He drove back up to the castle and found Sydney in the great hall speaking with Samantha's brother, Dalton.

Dalton Moore was ex-FBI, and he and his buddy Colton ran the human side of security for the royals. Dalton apparently owned several car dealerships back in Georgia, which, along with his salary from Kade, made him a wealthy man. With his model good looks and southern accent, Thane knew the women flocked to him.

Right now, he was smiling at Sydney in a way that irked Thane, and he walked quickly to her side, wrapping an arm around her waist and kissing her temple. "Hi."

She grinned up at him. "Hi, honey. Have you met Dalton?"

"Aye." He shook Dalton's hand and forced a smile.

"I was telling Sydney that if you can't get answers from the local cops, I can call a few contacts back in D.C. They'll be able to get to the bottom of her mother's accident."

Sydney slid her hand into Thane's back pocket. "Dalton says they can put pressure on the powers that be to tell them more than they're telling us."

"That's a generous offer," Thane said, carefully. "We'll be sure to let you know if we run into issues."

"Sounds good. I'm gonna go see my nephews for a bit, then head out. It was nice to meet you, Sydney."

"You too, Dalton."

The American left and Sydney faced Thane. "Chill."

"I'm sorry?"

She grinned and slid her hand to the back of his neck. "You went all squirrely with Dalton. You aren't jealous, are you?"

Thane sighed. "Admittedly, a little."

She giggled. "Silly man."

"Aye, lass. I am."

"Kiss me so I can make you feel better."

He leaned down and touched his forehead to hers. "I'd rather take you back to bed."

"Even better. We've got a few hours before we have to get ready for dinner, so let's go slay that jealousy dragon."

Thane laughed, kissed her quickly, and then took her hand and led her to bed.

* * *

"Did you ask what we could bring?" Sydney buckled her seat belt and set her purse on the car floor.

"We don't need to bring anything, love."

"Honey, we should at least bring a bottle of wine. It's rude to show up empty handed."

Thane turned to her and raised an eyebrow. "Niall is arguably my closest friend outside of you, and I highly doubt he will care if we don't bring a bottle of cheap wine."

"It's a good thing we're going to stop at the store and buy an expensive one, then, isn't it?"

"We're already late, Sydney."

She sighed. "It's rude, Thane."

He shook his head and unbuckled his seat belt. "Give me a second."

Thane jogged back into the castle, returning a few minutes later with two bottles of wine, one red, one white. He climbed back in the car and handed them to Sydney. "Okay?"

"You did not just go and steal wine from the king, did you?"

"No, lass, I borrowed them. I'll be replacing them tomorrow. And you'd better be happy...the red's going to cost me six hundred pounds to replace."

Sydney gasped. "Go put it back."

Thane turned the car toward the drawbridge with a smirk. "We don't have time to put it back."

"I'll pay for it."

"What?"

"I'll pay for the wine."

"Like hell you will," he snapped.

Sydney rolled her eyes. "I insisted we have it. *I'll* pay for it."

"You will not."

"Thane, I have inherited a great deal of money from my parents, which I rarely get to spend. And once you and I combine our finances, it'll be more money that either of us can spend in a lifetime, so a couple bottles of wine is no problem."

He pulled the car over to the side of the road and took her hand. "You'll no' be payin' for the wine, Sydney. Yer me mate and it's my job to pay for things now, ye ken? I'll be hearin' no argument from ye, lass."

Sydney bit the inside of her cheek in an attempt not to giggle. "Ye ken? What does 'ye ken' mean? Are you turning into Tarzan, mister movie star?"

"Shite." Thane took a deep breath and shook his head, her touch calming him. "Sorry, love."

She widened her eyes. "What *was* that?"

"Remember when we talked about how mates take on attributes of each other after bonding?"

Sydney nodded.

"I think your passionate nature has become just as strong in me, and I'm feeling things I'm not used to feeling. It's strange, really." He squeezed her hand. "Intense. Overwhelming."

She giggled. "I get it. I'm sorry if I upset you."

"You didn't upset me, love. I just don't want you thinking you have to pay for things."

"But I really don't mind. Although, I guess our money's kind of each other's anyway, right, so it's silly of me to separate it.

Chalk it up to not being used to having a partner."

"We'll figure it out," he promised.

Sydney smiled and leaned over to kiss him. "This bottle of wine better be *really* good."

"Oh, 'tis, love." He kissed her again. "It's actually my favorite."

"Of course it is."

He chuckled as he pulled the car back onto the road.

"Is 'ye ken' like a form of 'you get me'?" She lowered her voice and waved a finger. "Like, big man hear me roar will be buying all things for you, little lady, do you get me?"

Thane laughed. "Aye, lass."

"Well, you better get a handle on that one, buddy." She let out a rather inelegant snort. "'Cause I'm no one's little lady."

"You are most definitely mine, Sydney."

"Oh, yeah?"

"Yeah."

"You are a ridiculous person," she retorted.

"Aye, but I'm *your* ridiculous person," he said as he pulled up to Max and Grace's home.

"Well, there is that."

Thane grinned and shut off the engine, climbing out and rushing to Sydney's side. After opening the door, he took the wine and kissed her once she'd climbed out of the car. "I love you, little woman."

"Suck it, big man."

"Oh, I plan to later."

She shivered. "Stop with the dirty talk or I'll ask Grace to give us a room."

He grinned. "The gauntlet has been dropped, love."

And I plan to suck and lick all manner—

"Oh my word, Thane Allen, if you start with the dirty mind talk while we're in the middle of dinner, I will kill you in the face."

Thane gave a mock gasp. "I had no idea I'd bonded with someone so violent."

"Well, remember our emotions being all out of whack? Yours might manifest in a weird old world Scottish accent, but mine turns into murderous tendencies."

Thane dropped his head back and laughed. "Bloody hell, you're adorable, lass."

"Murder's adorable to you? Oy vey."

"Love you, sweetheart."

Sydney grinned and wrapped an arm around his waist. "Love you too."

He kissed her gently and they made their way to the front door.

* * *

Sydney heard the buzzing of her phone and groaned as she snuggled closer to Thane. Finally, the noise stopped, but not for long. Adding to the din was Thane's generic ringtone, some annoying classical song that Sydney found grating. "Make it stop," she begged, and he did...sort of.

"Thane speaking." She felt his emotion and sat up with a gasp. Thane pressed the speaker key and sat up as well. "Aye, Cary, we're both here."

"Is everything okay, Uncle Cary?" Sydney asked.

"No. Lucy's been kidnapped."

"What?" Sydney grasped Thane's arm. "How do you know?"

Cary let out a ragged sigh. "The bastards sent a demand."

"Tell me everything." Thane set the phone on the nightstand and slid from the bed.

"They want to speak with Sydney. Face-to-face and alone."

"That's not bloody well going to happen, Cary," Thane ground out as he pulled on clothing.

"I understand. I'm just telling you what the demand is." Sydney's uncle sighed. "They know you're in Inverness and have given a deadline of tomorrow morning, five a.m."

"Shite."

"They're going to kill my little girl." Uncle Cary's composure slipped. "Just a moment."

The phone went silent and Sydney jumped off the bed and rushed around grabbing things to wear. "We *have* to go, Thane."

"I'm not putting you in danger, Sydney."

"You'll be there."

"He said alone, love."

Sydney pulled on a pair of jeans and then a T-shirt. "Well, we'll make it look like I'm alone. I have skills now, honey. Cauld—"

"Sid," Thane hissed, and pressed what she assumed was the mute button on his phone.

"Sorry," she said. "But let's think about this logically. I have Cauld Ane skills."

"And if he or they decide to meet you someplace that's too hot for you?"

She bit her lip. "I didn't think of that."

Now that she had gone through the conversion, she couldn't be anywhere over sixty-eight degrees. If she was, her body would begin to break down and blister, and she would die if the temperature rose much past that.

"Right. It's not going to happen."

"It's winter, Thane. How hot could it possibly get?"

"Thane?" Uncle Cary cut in.

He tapped his phone again. "Aye, we're here."

"We've set up a central control situation at my office downtown."

"We'll be there in less than two hours," Thane said, and hung up.

"How are we going to get to Uncle Cary's London office in less than two hours?" Sydney challenged. "We have to buy tickets, get to the airport, and then traffic—"

"Private plane, Sydney."

"You have a plane?" she squeaked.

"Max and Niall do."

"Oh, that makes sense." She sat down and pulled on her boots. "They won't mind us using it?"

"No, love." He smiled and grabbed his phone, raising it to his ear. "Nye? We've got an emergency and wondered if the plane's available. Aye. Wonderful. Thank you, brother. I'll fill you in when we're in the air. Aye. All right. 'Bye." He hung up and nodded. "All set."

"You have very useful friends," Sydney said.

Thane chuckled. "Aye, lass, I do."

They finished dressing, left word with one of the house staff of their departure, and headed to the private air strip. Niall had obviously called ahead, because the plane was waiting for them, along with pilot, copilot, and two flight attendants.

"Mr. and Mrs. Allen, welcome," a pretty blonde woman in dark blue uniform said as they walked onto the plane. "I'm Nell, should you need anything." She turned to her left. "This is Zara."

"Lovely to meet you both," Thane said, and settled his hand on Sydney's lower back. "If we could have breakfast and coffee as soon as possible, we'd appreciate it."

"Of course, sir," Zara said.

Thane guided Sydney further into the plane and she took in the space. It looked like a comfortable living room more than a plane. A huge sectional that was bolted to the floor took up most of the middle of the plane, and there were side tables secured for takeoff and landing, but that could be pulled out and moved as needed. A wet-bar and fridge ran along part of the west side of the plane with cabinets above.

There were twelve seats with seat belts in the main part, and fold-up seats against the back wall, similar to flight attendant seats, if there were extra passengers.

"Wow," Sydney whispered as she sat in one of the window seats.

Thane sat next to her. "It's lovely, eh?"

"Yes, but you know if I get used to this, it'll be the only way I'll want to travel."

He chuckled. "I'm with you on that, love."

Zara arrived with two cups of coffee, cream, and sugar, and Sydney almost kissed her. "Thank you."

"My pleasure, ma'am." She smiled. "We'll serve breakfast after takeoff, but I do have some pastries if you don't think you can wait."

"Yes, please," she and Thane said in unison, and then laughed.

"I'll be right back." Zara walked away and returned seconds later with fresh blueberry muffins.

"Thank you," Sydney said.

Thane only smiled, considering he already had a mouthful of muffin.

"Hungry?" Sydney asked with a giggle.

"Starving," he admitted, once he swallowed.

Sydney ate a little slower, but no less enthusiastically. It was the best muffin she'd ever had, but that brought worry as to what Lucy was doing. Was she eating? Thane laid a hand on her knee just as Zara collected their trash, and then it was time for takeoff. Sydney didn't mind flying so long as she didn't look out the window, but takeoff was a little nerve wracking, so she gripped Thane's hand until the plane was in the air.

Once they leveled off and the captain said they could remove their seatbelts, Thane suggested they watch a movie and they settled themselves on the sofa. But before they did that, he called her uncle, who still didn't have an update. Thane promised they'd be there well before the deadline. He then called Niall and filled him in, all the while keeping contact with Sydney.

It was surreal "hanging out" on a plane. Sydney really did think she'd be ruined for commercial flights going forward, but for the moment, she was content to snuggle up against her mate and relax while the pilot flew them to London.

By the time the instruction to take their seats in preparation for landing came, Sydney was a little bit shocked. "Is it really time to land?"

Thane chuckled as they made their way to the window. "Aye, love."

"Can we keep going? Maybe to Fiji?"

"If you want to go on a vacation, baby, I'll take you," he promised.

"In this plane?" she asked hopefully.

Thane laughed. "I'm sure we can talk to Max and Niall about it."

She clapped her hands. "Awesome."

"But not Fiji."

"Oh, right. Crap." Her face brightened. "Alaska?"

"Perfect."

Worry hit her full in the chest and Thane reached for her again, but she moved away. "Oh my word, Thane, you did that! You've been doing it the whole time," she accused, realizing he'd not let go of her since they'd gotten to the plane, and she'd essentially forgotten about Lucy for the entire length of their flight.

"Aye, lass, I wanted you to feel peace."

"So, you block my worry enough that I'm planning some romantic rendezvous instead of being concerned about the fact my cousin has been kidnapped?" she snapped. "You're an ass."

"I'm an ass because I don't want you to worry?"

"Yes. I need to be focused on her, Thane. Praying for her, not forgetting she's in trouble and probably scared out of her mind."

He sighed, holding his hand out to her. "I'm sorry, love. I just hate when you're in pain. I will tone it down."

"Tone it down, how?"

"You won't forget the situation, but I can take some of the heartache away."

She stared at him for several seconds, before linking her fingers with his again and leaning against him. "Do you think we'll find Lucy?"

"Aye, love, I think we will."

"What if we don't?"

He reached across to cup her cheek. "We will."

She took a deep breath and closed her eyes. *Promise?*

Promise, love.

The plane landed and Sydney followed Thane down the stairs, climbing into an SUV waiting on the tarmac.

Sydney wouldn't let Thane comfort her on the way to Cary's office. She'd rather worry herself into a migraine than forget for a second that her cousin was in trouble. Lucy must be terrified, and since they didn't know who or what the threat was, it was even more dangerous. "Enough," Thane snapped, and Sydney jumped. He reached for her hand, holding strong even when she tried to pull away. "I'll no' have you this wound up, love."

"She would have to be if it was me in her situation."

"And if she were bound to a Cauld Ane, her mate would insist on calming her as well."

Sydney tried to pull away again, but he shook his head and she scowled. "Thane."

"No, Sydney, I'll no' budge on this."

"Bossy, alpha-male, kilt-wearing—"

"Careful, lass," he interrupted. "You complain once about the kilt, you'll no' be seeing me in one again, and I know how much you like it."

She forced herself not to smile. "Suck it."

"We're going to find her, Sydney."

"I hope so." She kept hold of his hand, but turned to look out the window, forcing her thoughts to stay focused on her cousin, at least enough to send up a prayer.

CHAPTER EIGHTEEN

SYDNEY'S HEART RACED for approximately one point two seconds as the car drove into an underground parking garage. "Thane, stop it."

"No."

She tugged at her hand, but it did nothing. She tried to counteract his Xanex mind tricks, but she was still too new to her abilities and, quite frankly, didn't know how to do it. She intended to find out though, and then he'd be sorry.

"No, you won't."

"Get out of my brain!" she snapped.

The car came to a stop outside a bay of elevators and Sydney reached for the door handle.

"Wait," Thane said, squeezing her hand.

"Why?"

He didn't answer as he stared down at his phone.

"Thane?" she prodded.

"I'm waiting for your uncle to give the okay."

"Screw that," she snapped, dragging her hand from his while he was distracted and pushing open the door.

"Damn it, Sid," he growled, and followed her. He grabbed her around the waist as she hit the elevator button and pulled her back toward the car. "If you *ever* do that again, I will take you over my knee."

She forced away the delicious shiver his threat produced and blustered, "You ever try that, and I'll cut you."

"Bloody hell. I'm no' havin' this fight with you right now, Sydney. You'll do as I say, or I'll bloody well tie you to a damn chair."

"You wouldn't!"

"I would. In a heartbeat." His eyes burned red and Sydney's mouth dropped open.

"I hate you," she rasped.

He held her tighter. "I'm fine with you hatin' me, lass, so long as you're bloody well alive."

She crossed her arms and refused to look at him. Thane stood rigid beside her, his heart racing and his arms tight.

"Now, Wallace," he said.

"Aye, sir."

Wallace led them into the elevator, then stepped in front of them. Sydney didn't struggle—there would be no point, but she did keep her arms locked and her emotions in their appropriate compartments.

Thane loosened his hold as they arrived at her uncle's floor and he stood waiting for them in the lobby. "Come with me," he said, and turned toward his office.

Thane laid his hand on Sydney's lower back and they followed Uncle Cary down the hall. Entering the office, Sydney noticed two of her uncle's top security men, Mathew and Nigel, standing by his desk. Once the door was closed, Thane released Sydney and she put distance between them, sitting in one of the chairs by the window.

"What do you have?" Wallace asked.

"We have one demand so far," Nigel said. "You're two hours early, so we're waiting for further instruction. He doesn't stay on the line long enough to trace him."

"So it's a man?" Sydney asked.

"The one who calls is, but we don't know if there's anyone else involved."

"Any indication as to where she might be?" Thane asked.

Nigel looked at Mathew, who shook his head.

"What are you doing right there?" Sydney demanded. "You better not be keeping stuff from us."

Sydney, settle.

I swear to Buddha, Thane, if you try to "handle" me, I will make you suffer.

Thane frowned, stepping to her and lifting her chin. *Do we need to take this outside? Because we have to find your cousin, and I get that you're angry with me, but we don't have time to hash it out, so you either stow that anger, or we take it outside.*

She pulled away from his hand and Thane turned back to the men. "So, do you know where she is?"

"No," Mathew said. "We heard something in the background, but we haven't been able to determine what it is.

"Can I have a listen?" Thane asked.

"Come with me," Nigel said, but before they left, Thane knelt in front of Sydney.

"We're going to find her."

Sydney rubbed her temples, the pain almost unbearable as she blinked back tears and nodded. A green haze hovered in her peripheral vision and she shook her head and blinked again.

"Take a few deep breaths, love, yer eyes are green." Thane took her hands and kissed her palms, easing her pain.

"What do you mean, they're green?" Despite the relief, she still scowled at him.

Your eyes are green. I think one of your gifts is manifesting.

"What gift turns your eyes green?" she snapped in a whisper.

I don't know, love, but we'll sort it out when this is over. He rose to his feet. *I love you, Sydney.*

She didn't respond as he left the room.

Uncle Cary made his way to Sydney and sat beside her. "How are you, love?"

"You're asking *me* that? Lucy's your daughter, you must be frantic." Sydney reached for his hand. "What does Auntie Clara say?"

"She's been sedated at home."

"I would imagine this would be upsetting."

"She was beyond upset, so we are helping her rest."

Sydney frowned. "Does *she* know she's been sedated?"

Her uncle lowered his head.

"Seriously?" Sydney shot out of her chair. "You're keeping her sedated without her consent?"

"It's only until we find Lucy. This way she doesn't know what's happening and when she wakes up, Lucy will be there."

Sydney let out a frustrated groan and stormed out of the office. She needed to run... or hit something; she wasn't sure which at the moment. Maybe both.

Her eyes flooded with angry tears as she rushed down the hallway. She needed to get away from all this testosterone-filled bullcrap that she was being subjected to. She couldn't believe her uncle would pull the same thing Thane was pulling; only using *actual* drugs to control her aunt. Sydney was disgusted.

Probably because she was distracted by being disgusted, she didn't notice Thane walking toward her. So when she felt an arm of steel wrap around her waist, causing her breath to leave her with an, "Ooof," she was taken totally by surprise. And when she was pulled into a small room that looked part supply closet, part shipping office, it took her a second to figure out what had just happened.

Without warning, she was pushed against the now closed door and kissed for all she was worth. She forgot that she was distraught and fisted her hands in Thane's shirt. Opening her mouth to deepen the kiss, she let the worry of the moment dissipate.

However, something Thane probably hadn't counted on was that her abilities were growing in strength. It didn't take her long to come to her senses and shove him away from her. "No!"

"You need to stop going down this bloody rabbit hole of despair, Sydney."

She stood by the door, one hand out to ward off her mate, and one at her chest, trying to catch her breath. "You need to stop trying to control me. It's not okay, Thane."

He swore, running his hands through his hair.

Sydney took several deep breaths. She felt her heart slow and her emotions calm. Once that happened, she folded. Sliding down the door to her bottom, she drew her knees to her chest and dropped her head as she burst into tears.

Thane sat next to her, but didn't try to placate her or control her emotions. He just sat there, his hands fisted on his raised knees while she watched him.

"What's happening to me?" she whispered.

He sighed. "The same thing that's happening to me."

"That's helpful, Thane. Thanks." She frowned. "Do you know what my uncle did to my aunt?"

"Aye, but only because I read it in your mind."

"He drugged her, Thane. *Drugged* her. She has no idea what's happening, because he is treating her like chattel. What if Lucy dies and Aunt Clara isn't awake to know about it? She will be devastated."

"I know, love. I don't agree with his methods, but I do understand the emotion behind it."

"I don't give a rat's ass about the emotion behind it, Thane. What he's doing is *wrong!*"

"Aye, love, 'tis. I agree with you."

"You do realize," she cocked her head, "that it's what you try to do to me."

Thane's eyebrows came together in a tight V and Sydney watched him as he processed her words. With a sigh, he held his hand out, palm up, asking rather than insisting, and she linked her fingers with his, the only movement she made to connect with him.

"I'm sorry, love."

She closed her eyes and nodded. "Thank you."

"We are obviously dealing with some emotional conflicts."

"Ya think?"

"I have a theory but until I can do some research, I'm not sure if I'm right."

"What's your theory?"

"It would seem we have similar gifts that are now clashing, which makes us stronger in all the wrong ways. You and I feel things on a level most don't." He lifted her hand to his lips and kissed it gently. "We need to figure out how to control our emotions and make them work for us, or we're going to find ourselves in a place where we might damage each other."

She opened her eyes and studied him.

"I don't want to hurt you, sweetheart. I'd rather cut off my arm than do that, and my heart breaks when you're upset. I find your pain affects me to my soul, and I'll admit I'm not handling it well. I'm so sorry, Sydney."

She couldn't hold on to her anger any longer, and she climbed into his lap as she burst into tears. "I'm sorry too, honey. I've never felt like this before, which isn't an excuse, but I feel totally blindsided by these emotions. They're overwhelming."

"I know, baby." He kissed her throat. "We'll sort it out. I promise. In the meantime, will you please let me work with your uncle's security to figure out what we're going to do? I will do my best not to keep things from you or treat you like chattel, but I'm hanging on by a thread here, and I can't worry about you and focus on finding Lucy at the same time."

"I can try, honey."

"Thank you."

She wiped her tears and took a deep breath. "Did you hear anything on the recording that might be helpful?"

"Aye. Water. Cary's sent men down to a few of the local piers and docks."

"Won't that take time?"

"Probably. They're starting with the Royal Albert dock."

"Why?"

"I don't know, love. I just have a feeling." He rose to his feet and held a hand out to her.

"What kind of feeling?" she asked as she took his hand, and he pulled her up.

"I can't explain it, which is one of the reasons I'm taking notice. I think our bonding has given me something I've never had before."

"Which is?" she prodded.

"Psychometry." He pulled her against him, wrapping his arms around her. "I touched something Lucy had given her father and was able to see or sense, I'm not sure, the dock. I'm running with it and praying it's the right direction."

Sydney settled her cheek against his chest and closed her eyes. "Me too."

"I'm going to kiss you now, love."

She let out a quiet giggle and lifted her chin. "Okay."

Thane kissed her gently and then led her out of the room and back to Uncle Cary's office. She took a seat by the window again, but kept a wary distance from her uncle. She was still beyond angry with him, but she needed to stay on point. It wouldn't help Lucy if Sydney went down an emotional rabbit hole.

Thane slid his hand to the back of her neck and squeezed. *Well done, love.*

She sighed. *Don't congratulate me just yet, Thane. I'm still pissed.*

Before he could respond, her uncle's office door was thrown open and a very angry, unusually disheveled and haggard-looking Clara Armstrong Ashworth stormed into the room, straight for Uncle Cary, where she laid a perfectly painful slap across his cheek. "You sodding bastard!" she screamed.

Thane pulled Sydney to her feet. "Let's give them a minute."

Sydney nodded and they left the room, along with Mathew and Nigel. Nigel ushered them into another office two doors down, but even with the door closed, the occasional four-letter word filtered through as Aunt Clara gave Uncle Carville the verbal thrashing of his life. Sydney hoped they would survive this... it was a betrayal her aunt wouldn't take lightly.

* * *

Lucy came to in stages. The pain slamming into her skull was something she'd never felt before, and her immediate thought was she was having an aneurysm. But then the memories flooded in and she bit back a whimper as she tried to open her eyes. She could only see through one.

"Well, there you are," Zach crooned.

"Zach?"

"Yeah, babe. Ya miss me?"

She swallowed, her throat raw. "Where am I?"

"Somewhere safe."

Lucy shifted and discovered she couldn't move much. She tugged on her hands and found they were bound tight. "What's going on, Zach?"

"Well, I'm trying to get your cousin to listen to what I have to say."

She remembered being in line at the coffee shop and then someone grabbing her from behind as she left and cut through the alley to get to the Tube. A twinge in her bicep brought back the memory of a brief but sharp pain and she remembered a needle jamming into her arm and then everything went black.

"I don't understand." Lucy still couldn't see him. She sensed he was behind her.

"That's because you're the dumbest bitch on the planet."

Lucy gasped. "What the hell?"

"Yeah, go ahead, get all pissy, Luce. It doesn't change the fact you're an idiot." He let out a cackle of a laugh. "And you're a really bad lay."

"What do you want, Zach?" As she tried to focus on his words, she took a look around her. There wasn't a whole lot to see. She was in a small, windowless room and the only source of light was an exposed lightbulb by the door.

"I want your cousin to get her head out of her ass and come take your place."

Lucy groaned. "Why?"

"Because she *owes* me."

"Can I please get some water?"

"No."

Lucy sighed. "Zach, I don't understand why you need to talk to Sydney, but we could have set something up."

"God, I can't believe you dumped me," he said as though he didn't hear her. "I just needed to keep you on the hook for a few more days, but no, you had to ruin the plan."

He slapped her on the head and Lucy felt like he'd hit her with a hammer. She cried out, even though she tried not to.

"None of this had to happen, Lucy. If Sydney had been as dumb as you, it wouldn't have. Now we'll see just how smart she is, because she's got twenty-nine minutes to show her face or you're dead."

"Why, Zach? What did we do to you?"

"You had nothing to do with any of this, Lucy. You were simply an avenue to get to Sydney."

"What did Sydney have to do with this then?"

He tsked as he came into focus. "That's for her to know, baby. It's gonna be our special connection."

Lucy licked her dry lips and tried not to shiver at the look in Zach's eyes. He was crazy. He was no longer the good-natured guy she'd met a month or so ago. He was a sociopath, and Lucy was in his clutches. She sent up a silent prayer of desperation as the black surrounded her again.

CHAPTER NINETEEN

THANE SET A bottled water in front of Sydney and cupped her cheek briefly as they waited for word from Nigel's men. Mathew had left the room about ten minutes ago and Sydney was on edge waiting for him to return. She took a sip of water, realizing just how thirsty she was, and sighed with relief. Maybe the fact her mate knew her so well was becoming more of a positive than a negative.

Thane's chuckle sounded in her mind and she scowled at him over her shoulder. *Nope, back to a negative.*

He leaned forward and kissed her gently. "Love you, baby."

She smiled. "I love you too."

Give me your hand.

She shifted her chair so they were next to each other and linked her fingers with his. He lifted her hand to his lips and kissed her palm.

Mathew returned and both Thane and Sydney stood quickly as he faced them. "Okay, we think we've found them."

"Who is it?" Sydney asked.

"Do you recognize him?" Mathew held his phone up.

"That's Zach," Sydney said.

"Aye," Thane confirmed. "Zach Miller. He and Lucy dated for a little while."

"You know his last name?" Sydney asked, surprised.

"Cary shared his findings after the background check. He wanted me to know before we met him for dinner. But your uncle had some concerns about the name and was looking further into him."

"And what did you find?" Nigel asked.

"Not much, honestly," Thane admitted. "Cary will know more."

Nigel looked at Mathew. "Do you think we've given them enough time?"

Mathew shrugged. "He'll want to know either way."

"I'll go and see," Nigel offered, and left the room.

Sydney leaned against Thane as they waited for Nigel to return.

Mathew checked his phone and pulled open the door. "We're free to join them."

Sydney led the group back down the hall and into Uncle Cary's office. She gave him a wide berth as she made her way to her aunt and hugged her. "Are you okay?"

"No, love, but I will be."

Sydney sat next to her and took her hand.

Uncle Cary's phone rang and everyone in the room went still. He put it on speaker. "Hello."

"So, Sydney's there," Zach said.

"Yes, she's here," Uncle Cary acknowledged.

"Hi, Sydney. Do you remember me?"

"Zach?" she said, playing dumb. Thane scowled at her.

What? He knows I'm here.

"Yep, it's me. Well done. I told Lucy you weren't an idiot."

Mathew held up a piece of paper he'd just written directions on.

"Is Lucy okay?" she asked.

"For now."

Another note and Sydney asked, "Can I speak to her?"

"She's a little tied up right now," he said, then laughed. "Literally."

Mathew held up another piece of paper and Sydney frowned.

"Zach?" Sydney asked. "Have you actually tied her up? Is she okay? Can she move?"

Seriously? She's tied up and Mathew wants me to ask him if she can move?

Just do as he says, Sid. He knows what he's doing.

"She's breathing, Sydney," Zach said. "She's fine, but she's not awake."

"Okay, what did you give her?"

"Question and answer time is over, Sydney," Zach snapped. "You have eighteen minutes to come here or she's dead. Your uncle has the address."

He hung up and Sydney rose to her feet. "Where am I going?"

"No," Thane said.

"I have to do this, Thane," Sydney stressed. "It's not up for debate."

No, Sydney, it's not going to happen.

It is, Thane. I can do this. You can be close.

"Shite."

"Can you take me?" Sydney asked Nigel.

He nodded and they headed out the door with her uncle. Thane followed closely and climbed into the back of the SUV with her. "I don't like this."

"I know, honey, but I'm doing it. You know I can handle it."

What if it's hot?

I won't do anything stupid, Thane. If it's hot, I won't go in. She grabbed his hand. "I can do this."

He clenched his jaw but gave her a slight nod.

"Thank you," she said.

"The building is on the right, Sydney," Nigel said, and pulled into a parking lot near the dock.

Sydney peered out the window at the shabby brick building and bit her lip. It appeared abandoned.

"You don't have to do this, Sydney," Thane said.

"Yes, I do."

"If you feel threatened at all, get out of there, okay?" her uncle said.

"I will, Uncle Cary."

Nigel pulled the car to a stop and turned to face her. "The door is closest to the water."

Sydney took a breath and nodded. "Right."

"Sid," Thane whispered.

"I'm okay, honey." She kissed him quickly and then climbed out of the car.

I don't like this.

She glanced back at the SUV and frowned. *I got it the first three hundred times you said it, Thane. Settle.*

She made her way around the building and found the door Nigel referred to. Squaring her shoulders, she turned the knob and pushed open the door. It appeared to be a boat house of some kind with an empty boat slip and not much else. She stepped further inside and the door slammed behind her, making her jump.

Sid?

I'm okay, I'm okay.

Shite.

I really am okay, Thane.

Another door opened across the building and Zach walked out. "Well, hello, dear sister."

"What?" she breathed out.

"Surprise! We're related."

"You're insane."

"I'm not crazy!" he screamed.

"Where's Lucy?" she demanded, trying to bring him back to the present.

"She's safe."

"Zach, I need to see her. I don't know what this is all about, but we're not talking any further until I see her."

What's the temperature, love?

It's fine, Thane.

"Well, come on, then," Zach said, and waved his arm.

Sid?

I'm fine, honey.

She followed Zach through the door he'd come out of and once her eyes had adjusted to the dim light, she located Lucy tied to a chair. "Luce!"

Zach grabbed her arm. "Don't."

"I have to make sure she's okay."

Sydney?

I'm fine, the temperature's fine... Lucy I'm not sure about. Just zip it for a bit.

"She's fine," Zach snapped.

Sydney wrenched her arm from Zach and rushed toward her cousin. Kneeling in front of her, she saw she'd been beaten pretty badly. "Lucy?"

Lucy groaned and raised her head. "Sid?"

"Hey, cuzzie. You doin' okay?"

Lucy licked her lips. "I'm so thirsty."

"Zach, Lucy needs some water."

"If I give her some damn water will you sit down?" he snapped.

Sydney took a deep breath. "Yes, if you untie her, give her some water, and let her go, I will talk to you."

Bloody hell, Sydney.

Thane...shut it.

"She stays tied."

"That wasn't the deal," Sydney pointed out. "You said you'd let her go if I met with you alone... and I'm alone, so you need to let her go."

"It's not even supposed to be her!" he screamed. "If I could have gotten you at Thane's house, this would all be over now!"

"You were at Thane's house?" Sydney frowned. "You were the one that night in the storm, smoking."

This would explain why we can't get a hit off the DNA, Sydney.

"No, that was the idiot I hired. Damn Europeans and their need for tobacco."

"Zach, you have to let her go," Sydney said again.

Zach let out a sigh of resignation. "I'm not lettin' her go, but she can have some water."

"But that's not what—"

"Shut up!" he bellowed. "Just shut up! She's not going anywhere."

He raised his hand and Sydney scowled. "You hit me and this is all over, Zach."

I'm coming in.

No! No, Thane, I'm okay. We're okay. Just give me some time.

"Bitch," he snapped.

"Let her go."

"No!"

Sydney swore and rose to her feet and Zach made his way to a small fridge.

"Pretend you're still tied," she whispered to Lucy while Zach has his back turned. Sydney made quick work with the bindings, grateful for her new Cauld Ane strength. Zach handed Sydney water and she helped Lucy drink it. "A little more," Sydney whispered, and Lucy sipped again. "That's it. Give it a minute and you can have more."

"Sit down, Sydney," Zach demanded.

He blocked the only way out, so Sydney did as he said. "What's this all about?"

"My sister's sick."

"Wait. You've beat the hell out of my cousin and you're threatening me because your sister's sick?" Sydney shook her head. "What do you *want*, Zach? Money?"

"I want justice."

"For what?"

"For my family."

"I don't understand," Sydney said.

"Your mother ruined our life!"

"*My* mother? What do you mean?" Sydney rose to her feet. "If you can't explain what's going on, I'm leaving."

"If you move, I will kill her." Out of nowhere, Zach produced a gun and pointed it at Lucy. "Sit down, Sydney."

Sydney did, but pulled her chair closer to Lucy, shielding her as much as possible. "It will help if you tell me everything," Sydney placated. "Start at the beginning."

Sydney.

You said I can heal myself, Thane, but I have to keep him from hurting Lucy.

I'm coming in.

No, you're not. Just give me a minute.

"Your mother wouldn't acknowledge the fact that she stole our money," Zach said. "It was ours, Sydney."

"I can't imagine why she'd steal money from you, Zach. We had our inheritance from my father."

"Which was half ours!" he screamed.

"What?"

"Your father is our father!"

"What are you talking about?" Sydney snapped. "You aren't that much younger than me, Zach. I would have known if my mother was pregnant."

"Maybe you *are* as stupid as your cousin," Zach said with a sneer.

"Screw you, Zach. You're not making any sense."

"The story goes that your father met my mother at a trade show in New York. She was young, naive, and had only been the States for ten years. Her parents were Chinese and spoke no English, so she had to translate the world for them. She was twenty and working as a maid at the hotel where he stayed that week, and he seduced her. That was twenty-four years ago."

"No, there's no way. My parents had been married for five years by the time they had me. They loved each other. He would have never cheated."

"Well, that's where you're wrong, big sis. He did cheat. When Mom discovered she was pregnant with me, he moved her out to San Jose. He bought her a house, one in a shitty neighborhood, because she wasn't his wife, and he wasn't going to bring his affair into Menlo Park."

"My mom wouldn't have stayed with him if he cheated. Your mom must be mistaken." *Or a liar,* Sydney thought to herself. Pain came and went quickly as Thane obviously helped ease her discomfort.

You're an empath, Sydney. You'll be able to tell if he's telling the truth.

Sydney listened a little differently as Zach spoke again.

"He was with us every other weekend and two weeks every summer, until he was too sick to keep up the charade. He'd come for our birthdays, but when he couldn't we had to celebrate alone. Then when he was in hospice, we had to sneak in to see him in the hospital. Do you know how many times we almost bumped into you?" He settled his hands on his head. "*God*, it was humiliating."

Sydney blinked back tears. "You're wrong."

"He promised us he'd take care of us. *Promised* we'd be okay." Tears welled up in his eyes. "But he lied! And your bitch of a mother refused to listen to us. Beth's dying and we don't have the money for her meds. Dad's life insurance was barely enough for the first six months of treatment."

"What do you mean my mother wouldn't listen?" Sydney asked, but the truth of what he was saying flooded in. The memories of her mother's cryptic phone calls at random times...the ones she always brushed off...settled in her soul. Her father *was* gone every other weekend and he always took two week-long trips during the summer, every year. Sometimes more on occasion, but always the same weeks each time.

"Dad promised he'd leave us money, but when it came down to it, your mother stopped it. We never got the big payout he'd promised, just the small one that my mother had paid the premiums under her name. Your mom knew, Sydney. I don't know how long she knew, but she sure as hell knew at the end, and made sure we got nothing. Dad had a contingency if that were to happen; I'd just never expected it would need to be used."

"What kind of contingency?"

"A little life insurance policy that would pay my mother should yours have an unfortunate accident."

"What?" she squeaked.

"One million dollars is going to be paid out as soon as the cops release your mother's body, but they're takin' a long damn time to do it, and Beth needs help now."

"How could you possibly have counted on—" She stopped herself with a gasp. "You! You hired the guy to kill my mom!"

He shrugged. "Did I? No one will ever prove anything."

"But if you're struggling financially, where did you get fifty thousand dollars?"

"Hypothetically, should I ever think to do something so reprehensible," he said, "I might consider borrowing from the money Mom got when she refinanced the house to pay for Beth's treatment. But that's hypothetically."

With a hiss, Sydney stood and headed for him. "You bastard!" she screamed. "Lucy, get down!"

Sydney heard a thump and Lucy's groan as she reached her arms out, Zach's body slammed against the wall and he let out a hiss of pain. She didn't realize she'd done all of that with her mind as she advanced on him again. She had little time to focus on what was happening, her murderous intent failing, as strong arms wrapped around her and pulled her away. Zach was summarily divested of his gun and shoved onto his stomach. He was cable tied and made to lie where he was until they were ready to move him. EMTs took care of Lucy as Thane dragged Sydney from the building.

* * *

"What are you doing?" she screamed. "Let me go!"

He held her tighter. "You can't kill him, love."

"Why the hell not? He killed my mom."

"I know, baby, but we need to find out more information... turn him over to the authorities."

"He gave us everything we need," she countered. "If we turn him over to the authorities, I can't make him pay."

"Sid." Thane cupped her face. Her eyes flooded with green, even the white, and Thane knew he needed to get her to calm down. "I need you to take a deep breath."

"Screw you."

He closed his eyes and concentrated on breaking down her defenses. She struggled against him, but he held tight. "Shhh."

"Thane!"

"No, sweetheart, you need to settle."

It took several minutes for her to stop fighting him, but he continued to hold her tight. He'd let down his guard before and she'd taken advantage of it, so he wasn't doing it again.

I hate you.

He grinned. "As soon as you calm down, love, I'll let you go."

"I'm calm."

"You're no' calm."

"I'm so calm, I'm Zen calm."

Thane chuckled. "Oh, my love, you're so far from Zen calm it's not even funny."

"*You're so far from Zen calm it's not even funny,*" she mimicked with a sing-song voice.

He dropped his forehead to hers again, listening to her heart. "Almost there, love."

It took a little while, but finally she fell against him with a sigh and wrapped her arms around his waist.

"There she is."

"I still want to kill him."

"I know, sweetheart," he whispered.

"He killed my mom."

"I know."

"My dad cheated on her." Her voice hitched on a sob. "She was the best person in the world, and he cheated on her."

"I know, baby."

"How could he do that?"

He took a deep breath and kissed her temple. "I don't know."

"I need to check on Lucy."

"She's on her way to the hospital. We can go in a minute." He rubbed her back. "I want to make sure you're okay first."

"I'm fine, Thane." She leaned back to look him in the eye. "Other than the issue of my overwhelming homicidal desires, I'm frickin' great."

Thane smiled. "All right, love, we'll go."

"Can we pass the bastard on the way?"

"He's gone, Sydney."

"What?" she snapped.

"They took him away."

She let out a frustrated squeak. "You did that on purpose!"

"Comforted you long enough for him to be taken to Scotland Yard? Aye, lass, I did."

"Jerk." Sydney pushed him away and made a run for the car.

Thane watched her go... waiting. She stopped midstride, bent at the waist, and settled her hands on her knees. He felt her frustration, but because she didn't like him interfering, he let her have her emotions...for approximately ten point two seconds. Then he moved.

Don't, Thane.

He stopped, but not until he was within a foot of her. *Sweetheart—*

No, Thane. I need a minute.

He felt powerless.

You need to get over it.

He shook his head. *Now who's in whose head?*

Sydney righted herself and faced him, crossing her arms. "Is this ever going to stop?"

"Your emotions being on ten?"

She nodded.

"It should." He sighed. "But this is all new for me as well, sweetheart, so I don't know how long it will take." Thane held his hand out to her. "You just need to trust me and let me help you calm down."

"I'm not good at playing the submissive wife, Thane."

"This isn't about submission, Sydney. It's about trusting me to know I have your best interests at heart and I'm protecting you. If I left you to your own devices while you were in that state, you would have killed him, and then where would we be? Hmm? You'd be in jail for murder and I'd be left without you."

She bit her lip and lowered her head, closing the distance between them and taking his hand. "It's always all about you, isn't it, mister movie star?"

Thane chuckled. "Damn straight."

Sydney closed her eyes and leaned against him. "I'm sorry."

"Baby, it's okay. This is all a learning process."

"I know." She smiled up at him. "But I'm sorry anyway. Even if I don't always show it, I appreciate you looking out for me."

He leaned down and kissed her. "I love you," he said against her lips.

"I love you too." She frowned. "Did I shove Zach into the wall?"

"Aye, lass."

"Without touching him?"

"Aye."

"How did I do that?"

"It appears you have the gift of telekinesis, so when you wanted him to move, you moved him."

"Wow." She let out a deep breath. "Do you have it?"

"Not yet. My strongest gift is suggestion, like when I put you to sleep. But it's something that will more than likely happen, just as you will more than likely acquire my gifts soon."

"Can we practice later?"

He smiled. "Of course we can. For now, let's go check on Lucy."

Sydney nodded and they walked to the car.

CHAPTER TWENTY

Arriving at the hospital, Sydney was relieved to discover Lucy wasn't actually in as bad of shape as she suspected. Bruised and battered, but nothing was broken and she didn't need stitches. Just ice, pain meds, and lots of rest.

Aunt Clara still wasn't talking to Uncle Cary, but managed a little civility until Lucy was released. Then the gloves came off and she insisted he stay at a hotel for a few nights until things calmed down. Sydney unwittingly caught the tail end of their argument as she was returning from getting coffee.

"Clara, love, don't do this."

"Don't you bloody well "love" me, Carville Ashworth. If you loved me, you wouldn't have tried to drug me. *God*, do you really think I'm that stupid? I was a nurse in another life, you idiot. I slid that needle out of my vein and the doctor didn't even notice."

He dragged his hands through his hair. "I was trying to protect you."

"No, you were trying to "handle" me."

"I'm sorry, Clara." He dropped his head in contrition.

"I'm not ready to forgive you yet and, no, I can't tell you when I will be. You'll be lucky if you're ever allowed back in."

"Don't say that."

"You'll give me space right now, Carville, or I'm calling a divorce attorney today and we'll be done with it."

Sydney decided to announce her presence by making heavier footstep noises as she came around the corner.

"Oh, Sydney, love. Thank you," her aunt said, and took her coffee. "I'll speak to you later, Cary."

Aunt Clara walked back into Lucy's room and Sydney followed, giving Uncle Cary a slight smile on her way in. Thane and Anson were chatting, so she handed them their coffees and sat next to Thane.

Two hours later, Lucy was cleared to leave and the family headed back to the Ashworth's home. Uncle Cary made sure Lucy was settled and then did as Aunt Clara asked him to...he gave her space, but left a team of security guards to watch the house. Sydney didn't want to leave her cousin, so her aunt offered her and Thane a room, and they took her up on it.

After climbing into bed, Sydney snuggled close to Thane as she tried to decompress after the most uncomfortable dinner she'd ever experienced.

"I thought Aunt Clara was going to stab Malcolm with her steak knife," Sydney whispered.

Malcolm Smith had been with Aunt Clara when she'd been sedated and was the one who'd driven her to the hospital when she'd waked up. Aunt Clara appeared to put almost as much blame on him as her husband.

Thane smiled. "I was ready if she tried."

"Aunt Clara has always been the sweet, fun-loving auntie. I have *never* seen her raise her voice. I'm not sure she and Uncle Cary are going to survive this, Thane. She's pissed."

"Aye, love, she is. But don't count him out just yet. He was wrong, but his intention was pure."

Sydney snorted. "Excuse me?"

He tightened his hold. "Hear me out before you hulk out on me."

She craned her head, unable to move the rest of her body. "You better explain pretty damn quick, Thane."

"Men are men, whether they are human or Cauld Ane, and sometimes we can be idiots."

"You got that right," she grumbled.

He smacked her bottom. "*But* there are carnal urges that overwhelm us on occasion, the biggest being the need to protect our women. So, no, I do not agree with what your uncle did, but I understand it."

"You understand him drugging her?"

"I understand him wanting to keep the pain away from her for a little while."

Sydney sighed. "I suppose I can see that side of it, but it really isn't an excuse, it's not even a good reason."

"I agree, love."

She relaxed against him. "Okay, mister movie star, you've calmed the beast."

He chuckled, rolling to hover above her. "I'm thinking I want to rile her up again."

"We're in a house full of people."

He kissed her neck and whispered, "We'll be very, very quiet."

* * *

One week later, Sydney was in their London apartment, attempting to throw together something that resembled dinner with the limited ingredients they had on hand.

They hadn't planned on staying in London as long as they had, but until the mess with Zach was cleared up, they couldn't head back to Edinburgh.

"Honey, I hope meatless spaghetti's okay," Sydney called as she peered into the refrigerator. "It's about all we've got."

Thane was in his office, trading e-mails with the powers that be (his words).

"That's fine, love."

Sydney let out a squeak and jumped, nearly hitting her head on the fridge door.

Thane chuckled. "Sorry, baby. I didn't mean to scare you."

"You move like you're walking on air." She wrinkled her nose and closed the fridge door, wrapping her arms around his waist. "I need to put a bell on you."

"As they say, everything can use more cow bell."

Sydney giggled. "That's so true."

"Do you want to eat first or talk?"

She leaned back to meet his eyes. "You have news?"

Thane slipped his hand into her hair and ran his fingers through it. "Aye, love."

"That doesn't sound good."

"I suppose it could go either way," he admitted.

"Let's talk first."

He nodded and led her to the sofa, where she sat facing him. He held his arm out to her. "Come here, love."

"So you can 'manage' me?"

He chuckled. "Protect, sweetheart. *Protect*."

She narrowed her eyes, but slid into his arms, settling her head on his chest. "It's that bad?"

"Zach's mother is here. So is his sister."

"O-kay."

"They want to see you."

"No."

He gave her a gentle squeeze. "That's what I told the police."

She glanced up at him. "*But?*"

"They didn't have anything to do with this, and Zach's mum is devastated that he did this."

"So?" She pushed herself up. "She participated in an adulterous affair, one that ultimately got my mother *murdered*. As far as I'm concerned, the whore can rot in a cell right along with her son."

He studied her.

"What? Don't you dare give me judgey eyes, Thane Allen! What kind of a woman has two children with a *married* man and then raises a psychopath? As far as I'm concerned, this is as much her fault as it is Zach's...or my father's. And believe me, if my father was here, I'd probably kill him all over again."

He raised his hands. "Baby, I'm no' judging you. You have every right to feel the way you do. But can I give you a little more information so you have the whole story?"

"Why? What would be the point? It doesn't change the fact my dad was a lying, cheating bastard, and it won't bring my mom back."

"Aye, lass, you're right."

"I'm not hungry." She rose to her feet. "I'm going to bed."

* * *

Thane let her go. This situation was far more intense and complicated than either of them had expected, and he knew she needed time to process. But he worried about the dark path she was going down.

He took a minute to pray and then he walked to their bedroom and slid onto the bed beside her, pulling her close.

"I can't believe you expect me to forgive them," she whispered.

He scooped her hair from around her face and slid it behind her back. "I'm no' asking you to forget or condone, sweetheart, just to forgive."

"I can't."

"I know you feel that way right now, love, and you're entitled to." He kissed her shoulder. "Be angry for a little while, hate for a little while... you have all the space to do that... but eventually, you'll have to let it go or you'll make yourself sick."

"Don't ever cheat on me," she whispered almost too quietly for him to hear.

"Sydney," he crooned, rolling her to face him. He wiped the tears from her cheeks and kissed her gently. "Even if it were physically or emotionally possible, I would never cheat on you. I won't leave you and I won't lie to you. I love you, baby. That will never change."

She burrowed into his chest with a sob. "I don't understand how he could do that to us."

"I don't either, love."

"And what kind of woman does that? She knew he had a family!"

"She actually didn't."

Sydney glanced up at him. "Zach said she knew."

"Aye, love, she knew, but not until several years in. He'd lied to her as well, and when she found out, she made a move to divorce him, which is when she found out they weren't legally married."

"I don't understand."

He stroked her chin. "He committed bigamy."

"Oh my word. Seriously?" She face-planted into his chest again. "He was such an asshole."

"At the risk of insulting the dead, I agree. On top of the fact your father was a sociopath and knew exactly how to work her, she's the type of woman who has no apparent life skills."

"What do you mean?"

"She's totally incapable of handling anything emotionally taxing, and she's been thrust into drama that's she's not prepared for."

"You mean life," she said, snidely.

"Aye, lass."

"And how is that an excuse?"

"It's no', love, but perhaps a little grace can be given, considering she has a limited grasp of the language and has been dealt a blow that could fall the strongest of people."

"I'm not very strong and it didn't 'fall' me."

"You are strong, Sydney," he argued.

She snorted. "Because sobbing snotty tears into your T-shirt proves that."

"Partly. But also partly because at twenty-four, you had to lay your mother to rest and deal with her estate by yourself."

"Uncle Cary took care of that," she countered.

"Oh, really?" He gave her a squeeze. "Did you no' read the documents that you had to sign? Did you no' agree to donate yer mother's organs without anyone there to lean on? Did you no' pack up your most treasured items and have them stored somewhere safe? Your uncle came to yer aid, aye, but he couldn't make the important decisions. You did that, love. You did it and you did it without a woe is me, or buckling under the pressure."

"No, I saved all that up for you and your T-shirts."

He chuckled. "Maybe you did, but it's mine and my T-shirts' privilege to take some of that pain from you. Don't doubt that I consider it an honor."

"Thane," she rasped as new tears started. "You make me sound amazing."

"You are amazing, sweetheart. And I think the fact that you are, means you'll find it in your big heart to give grace and mercy to a woman who doesn't have a clue what happened to her life."

She groaned. "I see what you just did there, mister movie star."

"Do you now?"

"I hate you so much right now."

Thane laughed. "I wouldn't be doing this right if you didn't."

She lay in his arms silently for several minutes before letting out a ragged sigh. "I'll think about meeting with her, but I'm not promising anything."

"I'm not expecting you to."

"Really?"

"Really, love. I've said my piece. I'll support whatever you decide."

She nodded into his chest. "Thank you."

"How about we order out for delivery."

"Mmm. Chinese?"

"Sounds perfect," he said, and kissed her gently before climbing off the bed.

She slid from the mattress and gave him a tired smile. "I'll just wash my face."

"Okay, love." Thane kissed her again. "I love you, Sydney."

"I love you too."

He left the room and headed for the drawer full of menus. A knock sounded at the door and he opened it in surprise. Wallace stood on the porch with a box in hand.

"Wallace?"

"Sorry sir, I hope I'm not disturbing you. Sydney's uncle received this this morning. It's addressed to her. We've scanned it and it's safe to open."

"Thank you, I'll let her know," Thane said and took it from him, closing the door. "Sid?" he called.

She walked into the room, pulling her hair up into a bun. "What's that?"

"Wallace brought it by. It was delivered to your uncle this morning."

Sydney read the shipping label. "It's from my mom's school. She taught art there." Tearing at the packaging, she pried open the flaps. She pulled out several small canvases painted in her mother's signature style.

"Those are lovely, sweetheart."

Sydney blinked back tears as she sifted through each one. "She was amazing."

An envelope floated to the floor and Thane scooped it up. Just one word, "Sydney," was written in her mother's handwriting on the outside.

Sydney set the painting down and ripped open the letter, unfolding it gently as she began to read: *Oh, my sweet girl, how I hope and pray you never see this letter. If you do, it means I'm gone and you're having to deal with all of this without me. I hope you'll lean on your Uncle Cary. He loves you like he loves Lucy and Antsy, and I trust he'll take care of you.*

There are some things you don't know about your father, and if I could take them to my grave, I would, but I now think he might have done something worse than cheating on us. Yes, honeybun, he cheated. He has two children with another woman, and I found out just before he went into hospice. I stayed because he was dying, and, believe me when I say I wanted to help him cross over into the next life much faster than he did, but we both decided to shield you from it. I wonder if it was the right thing to do, but it's done, and I pray you are okay and that you know how much I love you.

I got a strange call a few weeks ago about an insurance policy in my name, and I haven't been able to find out much more. I think now it might have been a mistake. But (as you know since you've walked in a few times), I have been getting threatening phone calls as well, and I wonder if this is far worse than we could imagine. The police are involved but nothing's been found out yet. Please don't be angry or hurt that I'm shielding you from this. I feel as though the less you know the better.

Sydney Roslyn Warren, you are the very best thing I've ever done... ever. You are the most remarkable young woman, and I don't credit myself or your father for that, it's you, honeybun. You are loving, smart, and beautiful all on your own merit. Never stop listening to your inner voice, never forget you are loved deeply, and always remember to follow your dreams, even if you're ninety-two and want to take a pole-dancing class... Sydney giggled through the tears...*you never know, honeybun, stripping in your elderly years might be your only option. But I hope and pray that you'll find a man who worships the ground you walk on, because he's the only man who will be worthy of you.*

I love you more than the stars in the sky and I know that one day we'll see each other again. I'll make sure my mansion's sparkling and tidy when you arrive. I love you, beautiful girl. Always. Love Mama.

Sydney dropped the letter as Thane wrapped his arms around her. She sobbed into his chest and he held her, saying nothing as the sadness washed over her. "She thought she was in danger."

"I know, lass. It's okay, I've got you."

Sydney let him comfort her this time, relishing the peace he provided. When she was sure she was all cried out, she decided to take a shower while Thane ordered dinner.

Walking out into the living room, she found Thane on the phone and he held an arm out to her. She slid into his embrace and leaned against his strong body.

"Aye. Oh, 'tis?" He chuckled. "Aye, Fi. That's quite accurate. I appreciate it." He chuckled again. "Aye, on so many levels. Right. Thanks. 'Bye." He hung up, slipped his phone in his pocket and pulled Sydney closer. "That was Fi."

Sydney smiled. "Yeah, I picked up on that. Who's Fi?"

"Fiona. She's the king's sister and she's become the unofficial expert on all things human-slash-Cauld Ane. I gave her a ring because I think your ability might have been recorded somewhere at some point and if anyone would know, she would."

"*And?*" Sydney ground out, and smacked his chest.

Thane chuckled and took her hand, guiding her to the sofa, and pulling her down beside him. "You are an empath, which is quite common among human and Cauld Ane alike. Where you're special...in an abilities way, not in the general sense of the word, since, to me you're the greatest gift I've ever been given—"

"Oh my word, get on with it, man!" she retorted.

He grinned and kissed her quickly. "You are what we call *ljós sannleikans*."

"Which means?"

"Truth revealer. You provide the light of truth." He raised her hand to his lips. "That part's not so common. In fact, there have only been six recorded Cauld Ane truth revealers in the past thirteen hundred years. It's why your eyes turn green and your emotions become overwhelming."

"And the green haze?"

"Aye, you'll see that in your peripheral."

"Why do your eyes turn red?" she asked.

"All Cauld Ane men have that, ah... reaction, shall we say... when we're angry."

She rolled her eyes. "Wow, that's so bizarre."

"It's actually quite amazing, love." He smiled. "And now that we know, we can work together to figure out how to handle it."

"Right now, can you handle feeding your mate?"

He nodded. "It's been here for ten minutes."

"Then you better dish it up there, buddy."

Thane laughed and went about feeding his mate.

* * *

Three days later, Thane drove Sydney down to Scotland Yard where Zach's mother and sister were supposed to meet them. They weren't sure if Beth would make it, as she'd been rushed to the hospital the night before and no one knew why or how long she'd be there.

Sydney gripped Thane's arm as though it was her lifeline as they made their way into the building. After separating briefly to go through the metal detector, she once again attached herself to him.

It's going to be fine, love. I've got you.

She nodded, but couldn't find her voice, internally or externally to respond. She felt like her emotions were on ten and her nerves were settled on the surface of her skin.

Let me help.

She bit her lip and glanced up at Thane. "Please." He smiled and within seconds, she was calm. She let out a relieved sigh. "Thank you."

He raised her hand to his mouth and kissed her fingers. "I love you."

"I love you too."

"Ready?"

She nodded and forced a smile as Thane opened the door for her and waited for her to precede him inside.

"Mr. and Mrs. Allen," Officer Smith said, and reached out his hand. "Thank you for coming."

Sydney thought it was interesting how the majority of the people who met them assumed they were married in the traditional sense and that she'd taken Thane's name.

It's going to happen, baby... and I am wearing your ring even though it's not "official."

I know. It's just funny.

He smiled.

"Right this way." The officer led them to a large, bright conference room.

A slight and nervous-looking Asian woman sat with a stunning young lady who did not look well. But she did look as though she'd made a monumental effort to look better than she felt. Both of them stood as Sydney and Thane walked in the room, and Sydney gripped Thane's hand again.

Deep breaths, love.

"This is Mei Wu and her daughter Beth," Officer Smith said.

Beth reached out her hand with a gentle smile and Sydney reluctantly shook it.

"I'm so sorry we have to meet this way," Beth said.

Sydney nodded and everyone took a seat as Officer Smith left the room.

"My mother doesn't speak much English, so please don't think her rude if she doesn't answer you," Beth said. "I'll translate, but I'm having a difficult time with my breathing, so I might have to take some breaks."

I want to be sick.

Thane squeezed her hand. *I've got you, love.*

"I'm not sure why you wanted to meet, to be honest," Sydney said.

"That was my idea, actually," Beth confessed. "I wanted to meet my sister. I think I was about seven when my parents split up, and I didn't know about you until I was thirteen, so you've always fascinated me. I'm sorry if this makes you uncomfortable, but if I could see our father just once more, I think I'd beat him with a pipe for what he did to us."

"It does make me uncomfortable," Sydney admitted. "Can I ask what's wrong with you?"

Beth nodded. "Ovarian cancer. I just finished chemo about two weeks ago, so I'm in a little bit of trouble for traveling."

"Then why did you?"

She sighed. "Because I wanted you to know that we're not these people. What my brother did is reprehensible. He has some mental health issues and for the most part, he's great provided he's on his meds, but we discovered he'd stopped taking them... right after he called to say he'd moved to London." Her mother said something to her and Beth responded in Chinese and then frowned at her before facing Sydney again. "Sorry. My mother feels we should keep this private. What she seems to forget is that it's already about as public as it can get and you deserve some answers."

"I appreciate that."

"Zach's sick," Beth continued. "Not that his illness excuses anything he's done. We will support whatever the courts decide to do, but he's not right. If he was, he would have never done this." She blinked back tears. "I don't really know who he is anymore. We've always been close, but this... this isn't something I can push past right now."

"I'm sorry, Beth," Sydney whispered. Thane ran his thumb across her fingers.

"No. I am." She nodded towards her mother. "And so is Mom. I know it's just words, but if she'd known about you and your mom, she would have never married our father. She would have never even gotten involved with him."

"I appreciate that."

"We'll do whatever we can to help," Beth said. "I don't really know how any of this works."

"I don't either," Sydney said. "Does your mother know that Zach used her money to hire the man who killed my mom?"

"We found out this morning. A check bounced."

"Oh," Sydney whispered.

"I'm so sorry, Sydney."

"You didn't cause any of this, Beth. I don't blame you."

"I appreciate that." Her mother said something again and Beth nodded. "I should really go back to the hotel and rest."

"Of course," Sydney said.

Officer Smith returned to the room and smiled. "We have the paperwork ready for you, Mrs. Allen."

"Thank you." Sydney rose to her feet and Thane followed.

"Don't get up, lass," Thane said when Beth moved to do so.

"I can't imagine what I can do, but if there's anything, will you please let me know?" Beth asked. "Officer Smith has my information."

Sydney nodded and led Thane out of the room. She didn't speak much as she read over and signed the charges against Zach, and she didn't speak much as Thane took her home. By the time they walked into the apartment, she was emotionally shattered. "I'm going to lie down for a little bit."

"Hey." Thane pulled her against him. "You okay?"

She nodded. "I just need to process."

"Okay, baby. You process. I'll check on you in a little bit."

"'K." She pulled away and headed to their bedroom, stretching out on the bed and quickly falling asleep.

* * *

Thane checked in with Sydney every few minutes. He felt her lose her battle with sleep, so he knew he could relax for a little while at least. He decided to make a call.

"Sir?"

"Wallace, I need you to do some background on Mei Wu and her daughter Beth."

"No problem."

"As soon as possible, aye?"

"Aye, sir."

"Thank you." Thane hung up and set his phone on the counter. He felt Sydney's fear and heard her scream a few seconds later, but he was already in their bedroom.

She was sitting up, breathing heavily until she caught sight of him and then she calmed. "Sorry."

He slid onto the bed beside her and pulled her onto his chest. "Don't apologize, love. It's been a tough day."

"You can say that again." She kissed his chest. "I liked Beth."

"I did too."

"I did not like her mother."

Thane chuckled. "You're entitled to feel that way, love. She was the woman who stole your dad."

"I don't know if I can believe she didn't know."

"Well, I can't imagine you can know. Only she and your dad really know what happened."

"Do you think I'm a bitch for not liking her?"

He lifted her chin. "Sweetheart, you don't have to like her. You met with her. You treated her with respect. No one can expect any more than that from you."

"My mom would," she whispered.

"I don't know that she would, love."

"I just don't want her to be disappointed in me. I don't know where my allegiance is supposed to lie."

Thane gave her a gentle squeeze. "Your allegiance lies with you and me now, love, and I've got you. I was so proud of you today. You were calm and sweet, and you didn't jump to any conclusions. You let Beth have her say, which was gracious of you."

"She doesn't look well, honey."

"I know."

"I think we need to help her."

He smiled. "I know that too."

"You already called Wallace."

"I already called Wallace."

"Man, I love you."

He laughed. "Love you too, baby."

"Can we go home now?"

"Aye, love, we can go home. How long do you need to plan a ceremony?"

"A week."

He lifted her chin again. "Are you serious?"

"Yep. We'll get Elspie on it and it'll be done in two days."

"You're probably right about that."

Sydney giggled. "One week."

"Aye, lass, one week."

He kissed her gently. "I'm starving. How about you?"

She sat up and straddled his hips. "Yes, but not for food."

"Let's feed you then."

"Good plan." She leaned down and kissed him, and Thane fed her until she was stuffed.

CHAPTER TWENTY-ONE

SYDNEY STOOD IN front of the full-length mirror in the bedroom she shared with Thane and studied herself in the brand-new wedding gown he'd insisted on buying her. He had a small obsession with dressing her in lace she'd discovered, and this gown didn't disappoint. The entire bodice was lace, embellished with tiny pearls and beading, and the cap sleeves were removable. A draped skirt flared out the back into a sweep train that could be pinned up to avoid tripping.

"You look amazing," Lucy said as she joined Sydney at the mirror.

"So do you."

Any bruises Lucy had left on her body were covered by her bridesmaid dress, and the ones on her face were light enough now to hide with makeup, so she looked like herself again.

"I have something for you from Thane." Lucy handed her a velvet box.

What did you do?

Nothing less than you did, sweetheart. Thank you for the flask.

Sydney grinned. *Thought you might need one to calm your nerves.*

Cheeky.

She opened the box to find the most exquisite necklace. A simple, but elegant white gold chain with a teardrop diamond that matched her earrings perfectly. *Honey, it's beautiful. Thank you.*

I love you, sweetheart. I'll see you in a few minutes.

I love you too.

"Ohmigod, Sid, it's gorgeous."

"Help me put it on, will you?"

Lucy grinned and helped her with the clasp while Sydney held her hair up. The stylist had suggested she sweep it into a side bun on the left side of her neck and, rather than a veil, she wore a lace flower embellished just like her dress. It was the perfect accessory to a perfect gown.

Elspie and Lucy were Sydney's attendants and Elspie joined them with a gift from her parents. "This was Mum's mum's mum's," Elspie said with a giggle and handed her a beautifully carved wooden box. "Us girls all got something from Mummy on our wedding day, and this is yours. I haven't seen it, so will you please open it right now?"

Sydney laughed. "You're so impatient."

"Aye, love, I am. Now open it."

She did, and the three of them put their heads together and let out a collective, "Ahh."

Inside sat an intricate silver bracelet that appeared to have been handmade.

"Och, lassie," Elspie said, excitedly. "It's Great-granny's bracelet. Her mate, um, husband hand-forged it before they sailed from Iceland. He gave it to her after their first son was born."

Sydney gasped. "It's stunning."

"Aye, 'tis. And it's almost a thousand years old."

"I thought you said it was your great-granny's," Lucy said.

"Give or take a few greats," Elspie improvised.

"Oh, wow," Lucy said. "You've saved things that old?"

"Aye." Elspie smiled as Sydney slipped it on her wrist. "It sits nicely next to the one Thane gave you, eh?"

Sydney blinked back tears. "It's perfect."

"No crying, cuz," Lucy ordered even as she dabbed at her eyes with a handkerchief. "None. Stop right now."

The ladies laughed and then Clara poked her head in. "How's my favorite niece?"

"I'm great, Auntie."

"Your man's ready for you, love."

Sydney nodded and followed her family downstairs and to the doors that opened onto their back garden. Her uncle waited by the door, and despite his tension with Aunt Clara (they were working it out), he was the man who loved her like a father. She couldn't have imagined anyone else walking her down the aisle.

He kissed her cheek and smiled. "You look beautiful, love."

"Thanks, Uncle Cary."

"Ready?"

She nodded, took her flowers from her aunt, and looped her hand through his arm. Niall led Aunt Clara to her seat and then it was time.

Sydney kept her eyes on Thane as she walked down the aisle and forced herself not to cry even though he was. They might already be technically married, but the day was still just as special and as they said their vows again, she sent up a silent prayer of thanks.

Thane had brought light into the darkest part of her life, and she couldn't have been more grateful. She was safe in the peace that their life together would be more than she could ever hope for.

"You may now kiss your bride."

Sydney grinned and raised her head as Thane stroked her cheek. "I love you."

"I love you too."

Their kiss sealed their vows and his love healed her pain. Life was finally perfect.

EPILOGUE

Three years later...

SYDNEY CRADLED HER one-year-old son, Ryder, to her chest as he tried to fight sleep. "You're just like your Mama, huh?"

She rocked him as she walked down the hall to the nursery and settled him in his crib. He tried to fuss, but she laid her hand on his chest and smiled. "No, baby. It's time for you to sleep. Sleep now, little man."

Sydney had perfected Thane's ability to "suggest," and she giggled quietly as Ryder's hands fell to the side and his eyes closed.

I've created a monster.

Oh my word, honey, this is the best power ever.

Not the telekinesis?

Sydney slid the blanket over her son using said power and bit her lip. *Okay, maybe it's the telekinesis.*

Thane's chuckle sounded in her mind. *I'm almost home. You best have my supper on the table, wench.*

She sneaked out of Ryder's room and pulled the door closed. *You're hilarious, mister movie star.*

She arrived downstairs just as Thane walked through the front door, pulling her into his arms and lifting her off her feet before she'd even stepped off the last stair.

"Och, love, I've missed you."

Sydney giggled, sliding her fingers through his hair. "It's been two hours."

"Aye, lass. Two long hours."

He lowered her to her feet and laid his hand on her belly. "How's our wee girl?"

"Right now she's doing cartwheels because she knows her daddy's close."

"Are you tired?" He frowned. "You should rest, love. I wish you'd let me hire someone to help."

"Thane," she admonished. "I'm two months away from delivery. I'm fine. Beth arrives in six weeks and with Elspie and your mom here every day, I'm flush with help."

Samantha had informed Sydney that because she shared a blood bond with Beth, she'd have the ability to heal her now that she was Cauld Ane. Sydney had met with Beth once more before she left for the States and Beth had let her know a few weeks later that the cancer had disappeared. It had been a medical mystery as far as the doctors were concerned.

Beth and Sydney had forged a tentative bond at first, one that had gradually grown into a sweet friendship that the sisters found to be greatly satisfying. They didn't talk about their moms or the sadness they had both suffered because of their father.

Zach had been sentenced to life without parole for the murder, plus twenty years for the kidnapping of Lucy. He'd been extradited to the United States, which meant his mother could visit. No one could rejoice in it, but it was at least some form of closure.

The man who'd killed Sydney's mother had never woken up from his coma, dying a few weeks after Zach's trial. Another sad end to a sad situation.

Thane wrapped his arm around Sydney's waist. "Well, come and put yer feet up now and I'll make supper."

"And fill me in on the council meeting?"

He smiled. "Aye, love. I'll fill you in on the council meeting."

Sydney folded herself onto the large suede sectional in the great room and watched Thane move around their kitchen as though he was born in it. "Why aren't you a celebrity chef?"

He laughed, setting steaks on the counter. "We're supposed to be lowering our profile, love, not starting new careers that will add to the fame."

"Oh, right. Stupid immortality, it screws everything up."

"Oh, I don't know," he countered. "I quite like the fact I'm going to see you every morning for the next several hundred years."

"Or thousand."

"Aye, lass. That would be better." He pulled open the fridge and brought a bottled water to Sydney. "Hydrate, please."

"Aye, bossy," she retorted.

He leaned down and kissed her gently. "More and more practice as the years go on, baby, remember that."

She grinned. "You never let me forget it."

"Well, that's true." He headed back to the kitchen and started his masterpiece.

"So, what was the final decision?" she prompted as she checked to make sure the baby monitor was on, setting it back on the table next to the sofa.

"We're all going underground for a bit. Everyone in Fallen Crown was ready to anyway, now that Ollie's found his mate, so we're all settled. I don't think we're going to make a big deal about it to the media. My people have told the press I'm focused on my family right now, but if I want to do another movie in the future I can. It's not unprecedented that someone who's in their "fifties" can't still be an action hero."

She wrinkled her nose. "Well, provided you age like Jason Statham, not John Travolta."

Thane laughed. "Sure, we'll go with that."

"What will we tell my family? Lucy's going to notice if I don't age."

"We'll cross that bridge when we come to it, eh?"

"Okay," Sydney said. "So what are we going to do with ourselves?"

"We're going to raise our children, run our charities, travel. Anything we want to."

She sighed. "It all sounds too good to be true."

"Does it?"

"Yep. Little bit."

"Don't fret, my wee worrier, our children will keep us plenty busy, especially considering you're going to give me six more."

She choked on her water. "You want me to have eight?"

"Over time, lass. Not all at once."

"Oh, that makes me feel so much better. Thanks, honey."

He grinned, walking out onto the patio and throwing the steaks on the grill. Leaving the door open, he walked back in and set the plate in the sink.

"So if the Cauld Ane are officially going underground a bit, what does that mean for us in general?"

Thane settled himself on the sofa next to her. "Not a whole lot, to be honest. We'll still have our parties and our celebrations; we'll just do it away from the public eye. Samantha's thrilled, let me tell you."

"I bet." Sydney giggled. "What about you? Will you miss the lights of the marquee with your name big enough for everyone to see?"

"I've never cared much about that, baby."

She smiled just as the timer sounded and Thane stood and headed back out to the patio to flip the steaks. "Are you worried about the decision?" he asked, sitting beside her again.

"Not unless it's going to rob you of your joy not to do movies for a while."

He squeezed her knee. "You're my joy, love. Ryder's my joy. And when she comes, Gertrude will be my joy."

Sydney choked on her water again. "Stop doing that to me," she demanded. "We're not naming her Gertrude."

"Well, we need to come up with something if you're not going to name her after your mother."

"Linda, honey. We can't name her Linda. It's an old person's name."

"I happen to know several people named Linda who aren't old," he countered.

"Well, maybe old's not the right word. But it was my mother's name, and it just doesn't fit with us, you know?" Sydney sighed. "I'm fine with it being a middle name, but I want something awesome for our daughter. Something as cool as Ryder."

"All right, lass. We've got time."

"Yep." She smiled. "We have two months."

"Aye, love, two months." He rose to his feet again. "Salad?"

"Yes, but can I make it?"

"You don't like my salad?"

She slid off the sofa. "Thane, your idea of a salad is lettuce and croutons."

"That's a salad."

"That's a *lazy* person's salad," she corrected.

He grinned. "I'll give you that."

"I know you will, because you love avocado and everything else I put in there just as much, you just don't want to cut it up."

"No, I'm better with meat."

She shivered, biting her lip. "Oh, yeah, baby, you are *so* much better with meat."

He kissed her quickly and gently smacked her bottom. "I'll show you what I can really do with meat later."

"Can't wait."

Sydney giggled as she made a non-lazy person's salad and Thane tended to the grill. She watched him doing something so incredibly manly and, dare she say, American, and she felt her mother smiling down on her. Thane was right. Her mother would be happy for her. Sydney had been blessed with a life far more wonderful than she deserved and she once again found herself sending up another prayer. Carrying the plates onto the patio, she kissed her mate and they sat down to enjoy a perfectly wonderful evening while their perfectly wonderful baby slept upstairs.

Life really was perfect.

I was born and raised in New Zealand. With an American father, Scottish grandmother, and Kiwi mother, it's no doubt I have a unique personality.

After pursuing my American roots and disappearing into my time travel series, The Civil War Brides, I thought I'd explore the Scottish side of my family. I have loved delving into the Cauld Ane's and all their abilities… I hope you do too.

I've been happily married and gooey in love with my husband for more than twenty years. We live in the Pacific Northwest with our two sons.

I hope you've enjoyed **Bound by Light**
For other titles in the Cauld Ane Series,
or to learn about The Civil War Brides Series, please visit:
www.traceyjanejackson.com

Find me on Facebook, too!
http://www.facebook.com/traceyjanejackson

If you'd like to read the book Thane and Charlotte's movie was based on, The Bride Price, it's free for download pretty much everywhere, so check your favorite online seller.

Made in the USA
Middletown, DE
30 July 2016